"I want you to put your hands on my chest and try to resist me."

Erica returned Kieran's smile. "Bet you say that to all the women you know."

"Just do what you're told without the commentary."

She gave him a sharp, one-handed salute. "Yes, sir."

He balled his fists against his chest. "Grab my hands, angle your body away and don't let me move."

"Fine, but don't expect too much."

"Keep going," he demanded. "You're not using your legs."

Scowling, she regrouped and tried again, and he continued to prod her. "Push harder. Don't let me back up. Pretend you're fending me off because your life depends upon it."

Erica unexpectedly stopped, straightened. Before Kieran could level his next command, she planted her mouth on his....

Dear Reader,

Let's face it, going to the gym isn't exactly number one on everyone's list of having a good time, particularly if you have a fondness for your sofa. Mine is pretty darn comfortable. Yet I've learned that even the relatively easy task of walking my two dogs a couple of miles every evening amazingly alleviates some of the stress and helps to clear my mind.

That particular concept actually aided in formulating *The Mommy Makeover.* I asked myself, what would an out-of-shape, hard-working, single mom do if given the opportunity to work out with a sinfully sexy and wealthy health club owner/personal trainer who attracts women like a two-for-one shoe sale? Aside from the initial answer—"I should be so lucky"—"run like the devil" came to mind. But when you throw a child's concern for her mother's happiness in the mix, running suddenly isn't an option. Not to mention getting caught does have its rewards.

I hope you enjoy this next O'Brien installment featuring Kieran, as well as the underlying themes of healing, acceptance, forgiveness and of course, love.

Happy reading (and exercising)!

Kristi

THE MOMMY MAKEOVER

KRISTI GOLD

Published by Silhouette Books

America's Publisher of Contemporary Romance

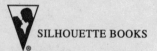

SILHOUETTE BOOKS

ISBN-13: 978-0-373-65438-3
ISBN-10:   0-373-65438-3

THE MOMMY MAKEOVER

Recycling programs
for this product may
not exist in your area.

Printed in U.S.A.

KRISTI GOLD

has always believed that love has remarkable healing powers and feels very fortunate to be able to weave stories of hope and commitment. As a bestselling author, National Readers' Choice winner and three-time Romance Writers of America RITA® Award finalist, Kristi's learned that although accolades are wonderful, the most cherished rewards come from networking with readers. She can be reached through her Web site at http://kristigold.com or at kgoldauthor@aol.com.

To my beautiful surrogate grandson, Connor Jarrett,
for reminding me of the simple joys
a child can bring to your life.

Chapter One

Only two things served to relax Kieran O'Brien—great sex and pumping iron. Since he still had several hours before he could leave work, and no special woman in his life right now, he'd have to settle for a weight session in his own private gym adjacent to his office. A sanctuary far away from the distractions and demands that came from owning two premier Houston health clubs, with a third location in the construction stage.

He strode through the club to the familiar sounds of expensive exercise equipment being put to good use, as well as a chorus of greetings from the regulars, several of whom were women he'd personally trained at one time. Some were women who'd wanted more than the standard workout. On the advice of those who'd groomed him to be a preeminent personal trainer, he'd vowed from the beginning not to mix business with pleasure. Not once had he crossed that line.

He'd kept his dating life separate from his professional life, in spite of the occasional temptation. The constant propositions had been one factor in his choice to halt private sessions; the other involved a lack of time. Not to mention a guy could only be so strong.

Kieran had almost reached his refuge across the room when a tug on the back of his T-shirt halted his progress and his plan. He expected a staff member announcing some minor crisis that needed his attention, or a patron inquiring about one of the latest innovations he'd purchased during a recent expansion. Instead, he turned to find a little girl with wide blue eyes and strawberry-blond hair, dressed in a pink jacket, white T-shirt and faded jeans, a denim backpack draped over her thin shoulder. She looked so sweet and innocent, all his irritation over the interruption melted away. Most likely she'd probably wandered from the play area and couldn't find her way back. A displaced kid he could handle.

"Are you lost, sweetheart?" he asked.

She shook her head and studied the floor. "I'm looking for Mr. O'Brien. Lisa told me he has kind of long dark hair and a lot of muscles and you look like that."

He quickly ran through a mental list of his employees but couldn't remember any Lisa. "I'm Mr. O'Brien. What's your name?"

"Stormy."

When she nailed him with a determined look, Kieran's gut told him she probably came by that name honestly. "Is your mom or dad a member?"

"I'm with Lisa and her mom."

Not a whole lot for Kieran to go on to locate a missing adult. "Who's Lisa's mom?"

"Candice Conrad."

Now that was a name he wouldn't soon forget. A typical

well-heeled, good-looking woman who had too much time on her hands and a disinterested husband, something he'd discovered when she'd hired him two years ago—and the reason he'd resigned from the position less than six months later. Not that his resignation had discouraged her from periodically asking if he'd consider taking her back on. "Do you need help finding Mrs. Conrad, kiddo?" A task he would assign to one of his staff members in order to avoid the overly enthusiastic Candice.

Stormy looked highly insulted. "I know where she is. I want to talk to you about buying training lessons."

He had to hand it to the kid—she knew what she wanted. And what she wanted was something he couldn't give her, even if she happened to be old enough to hire a trainer, which she wasn't.

Determined to let her down easy, Kieran guided her to a round table at the juice bar in the corner, away from the hum of treadmills and the whir of recumbent bikes. After he retrieved a cup of fruit juice and set it before her, he took the seat opposite hers. "How old are you, Stormy?"

She shrugged off her denim backpack and laid it on the table. "I'll be eleven two weeks before Christmas." She sent him a toothy grin. "My mom says I was her best present ever."

Considering her small stature, he would've guessed her to be at least two years younger. "You have to be eighteen to have personal-training sessions, but you could join our after-school youth exercise program."

She took a quick drink then wrinkled her freckle-spattered nose. "I don't want you to train me. I want you to train my mom."

A request he couldn't honor, but he could still be of some help. "Just have her call the club and ask for me. I'll make sure she gets a good trainer."

She looked at him as if he'd lost his mind. "That won't work. I want it to be a surprise for her birthday. And I want you to do it because Lisa's mom says you're the best trainer around."

Funny, Lisa's mom hadn't seemed all that interested in his fitness skills. "Look, Stormy, personal training is expensive and—"

"I know that." She unzipped her backpack, pulled out a fistful of crumpled bills and held them out to him. "I saved up all my allowance. It's almost eighty dollars. That should pay for a month, right?"

That would seem like a lot of money to a ten-year-old kid, but that amount didn't even cover an hour of Kieran's standard fee. "Tell you what. I'll give your mom a three-month membership for free. How's that?"

Now she looked completely dejected. "After school I go to the spa where she works, and I heard her tell the ladies that someday she wanted to hire a personal trainer, when she had some extra money. That's why I have to do this for her."

Kieran wasn't sure how he was going to handle the situation without totally crushing her. But before he could come up with a strategy, she added, "I just want her be happy again, like before."

The abject sadness in her voice had the impact of a punch in the chest, right around the area of Kieran's heart. "Before what?"

He saw the first hint of tears in Stormy's eyes. "Before my dad died six years ago. She still misses him. I miss him, too."

Her tears didn't fall, but something deep inside Kieran did. If he had even a scrap of common sense left after her heartfelt pleas, he'd turn her down gently and turn her away. But despite the shrewdness he'd developed over ten years as a business owner, regardless that he'd grown cynical when it came to people's intentions, along came a child to remind him that not everyone had questionable motives. Not everyone had been blessed with an easy life, either.

She sent him another pleading look. "If you need more money, I can give you what my grandparents send me for my birthday and Christmas. I can save more lunch money, too. I could sell my bike if I have to."

Even though he might regret it later, Kieran couldn't refuse her now. He also couldn't have her giving up everything, either. Not when it seemed she'd already given up too much.

After he took the bills she still clutched in her hand— money he planned to return to her later—he said, "This should be enough for a month."

Finally, she smiled. A smile that was bound to break more than a few teenage boys' hearts in a few years. "Since I can't get her to come to the gym, you can come by our house tonight and surprise her."

Apparently she was intent on running the show, and his schedule. He still couldn't help admiring her resolve. "What about tomorrow night?"

She took another drink of the juice. "She works late on Friday, but she comes home early on Thursdays because it's pizza night."

Unfortunately he'd already agreed to have dinner with his family at his sister's place this evening. But so what if he was a little late. His mother, a living monument of compassion, wouldn't only understand; she'd congratulate him. He'd just stop by Stormy's house first, which led to another question: "Where exactly do you live?"

She pulled out a piece of folded paper and handed it to him. "This is my address and my phone number, but don't call first. I want it to be—"

"A surprise." One he hoped didn't earn him a boot on his

butt delivered by a mom who might not take too kindly to her kid "buying" her a fitness program—unless Candice had cooked up some scheme with one of her wealthy friends, using a child as a pawn in an effort to bring him back into her life again. He wouldn't put it past her to stoop that low. Only one way to find out.

Kieran studied the address and found that the neighborhood wasn't far from his parents'—an area that included strictly middle-class housing, not manicured mansions. Apparently his suspicions about Candice's manipulation were unwarranted for a change.

After he tucked the paper away in his pocket, Kieran considered how he would react if his nieces approached someone they didn't know, and opted to issue a mild caution. "I'll be there, as long as you promise not to give out your personal information to strangers from now on."

She grinned again. "I promise, but you're not a stranger anymore."

He came to his feet and pushed the chair beneath the table. "You probably should find Lisa's mom now, in case she's looking for you." Before she came looking for Stormy and found him.

Stormy stood, rounded the table and gave him a quick hug. "Thank you, Mr. O'Brien."

When he noted the gratitude in her expression, he recognized he was doing a good thing. "You're welcome, and you can call me Kieran."

"My mom's name is Erica." Her smile faded into a frown. "You are going to come, aren't you?"

No way would he let her down now. If he could give this little girl and her mother some peace of mind, he saw no real reason not to make an attempt. "I'll be there around six, if that's okay."

"That works great." She turned and began to walk backward, another bright smile plastered on her face. "This is going to be the best pizza night ever!"

Erica Stevens had never seen such a pretty pizza delivery boy. Pizza delivery*man,* she corrected. A buff, patently gorgeous man with longish wavy dark hair and near-black eyes. Over six feet of pleasantly disreputable-looking, prime male flesh standing on her doorstep, wearing a pair of jeans and a black polo covered by a beige jacket—and not a pizza box in sight.

Of course not. The pizza never arrived in less than an hour, let alone five minutes after she placed the order. And generally speaking, pizza delivery guys were lanky high school students, not action heroes come to life.

For the sake of caution, she kept the screen door latched securely, at least until she knew exactly who he was and why he was there. "May I help you?"

"Are you Erica?"

Okay, maybe he was a new hire at the restaurant, they had prepared her order in advance and the box was still in his car because he wasn't sure he had the right address. "Yes, I'm Erica. Are you the pizza deliveryman?"

He leaned a shoulder against the white column supporting the porch and slid his hands into his jeans' pockets. "No. I'm your birthday present."

Erica's gaze immediately drifted to his jacket's pocket etched with the words Bodies By O'Brien. Surely not. Then again, she wouldn't put anything past her coworkers down at the day spa. "Please tell me you're not a stripper."

He cracked a dazzling grin, his teeth flashing white against the shadow of stubble surrounding his mouth. "I'm a personal trainer. My name's Kieran O'Brien, owner of Bodies By O'Brien, which is a health club, not a strip club. Or a pizza joint."

None of this made any sense to Erica. Not the circumstance

or her slightly warm reaction to his smile. She had the strongest urge to step onto the porch, strip off his jacket and see if his physique lived up to her expectations. Instead, she tugged her oversize sweatshirt down to conceal her obvious physical flaws. "First of all, my birthday is a couple of weeks away." Her thirty-first birthday, which she'd just as soon forget. "Secondly, I don't want a personal trainer."

He shifted his weight slightly, showing the first signs of discomfort. "Not according to the party who hired me. In fact, she said you've mentioned you'd like to have a trainer. That's why she's giving my services to you as a birthday gift."

Erica should've known she would rue the day she'd admitted that to Bette, the self-appointed salon matriarch. "I truly appreciate the gesture, but honestly, I'm a massage therapist at a busy day spa and I work crazy hours. I don't have a lot of extra time on my hands."

"You don't have any breaks?" he asked, his voice laced with suspicion.

"I usually don't get home until after 6:00 p.m., and I work Saturdays. The rest of the time I spend with my daughter."

He scrubbed a palm over his chin. "What time do you go into the spa in the morning?"

She could predict where he might be trying to lead her, and that was a road she didn't care to take. "I arrive around 9:00 a.m., but I don't do mornings well, Mr. O'Brien."

"It's Kieran, and a good workout gets the adrenaline going to carry you through the rest of the day."

"That's why they invented coffee."

"I never touch the stuff. I prefer a natural endorphin high."

She preferred a double espresso mocha cappuccino with whipped cream. But she did remember those endorphin days fondly, during a long-ago time when she'd been an avid gymnast. Back when she hadn't been toting thirty extra pounds and the weight of serious responsibilities on her shoulders. "Again, I'm not a morning person."

Kieran inclined his head slightly and leveled his gaze on her. "If you try it, you might like it. But if mornings won't work, we could come up with another plan that suits your schedule. No sweat."

And if she agreed, Erica assumed sweating would be a major part of the deal. She was already beginning to perspire despite the forty-degree November weather, and he hadn't even put her through a workout—at least not beyond the dubious one playing out in her imagination. "As tempting as that sounds, I'm afraid I'll have to decline. But I'll be sure to let Bette know that I appreciate the thought."

Now he looked confused. "Sorry, but I don't know anyone named Bette."

This was getting stranger by the minute. "Then who sent you?"

"You're here, Mr. O'Brien!" came from behind Erica right before Stormy unlatched the screen and rushed onto the porch. Suddenly, it was very clear how this man ended up on her doorstep, although the details were still sketchy.

"I take it you two know each other," Erica said, after her daughter finished giving Kieran O'Brien a voracious hug.

Stormy grinned, looking altogether pleased with her little surprise. "Happy birthday, Mom!"

She had no clue how Stormy could have possibly hired this man. Personal trainers were costly, and her daughter simply didn't have any real monetary resources. "It's not my birthday yet, and would you care to explain how you managed this, young lady?"

"Lisa's mom told me about Mr. O'Brien today when she took us to the gym. That's when I hired him." She glanced up at Kieran with pure adoration. "Isn't that right?"

He patted her cheek. "That's right."

Erica was surprised that Candice Conrad, who'd barely given her the time of day aside from arranging playdates for their daughters, had some role in this plan. Or *Candy,* as her friends called her. Ironic, considering the woman had probably never eaten an ounce of chocolate in her entire life. Or if she had, she'd managed to surgically remove the effects. But that wasn't exactly fair. After all, Candy dropped Stormy off at the spa almost every afternoon after school. For that reason, Erica should be a bit more benevolent. Then again, Candy had obviously taken it upon herself to impose her own fitness standards on poor, overweight Erica.

Regardless, Erica still had questions to ask Kieran O'Brien…alone.

After opening the door, Erica pointed inside. "You need to finish your homework before the pizza arrives, sweetie."

Stormy scowled. "But, Mom—"

"No arguments, Stormy. I need to talk to Mr. O'Brien for a few minutes."

"To set up the training sessions," Stormy said with certainty.

To tell him thanks, but no thanks, something Erica chose not to mention at the moment. "We'll see. In the meantime, your homework is waiting."

Stormy walked back into the house in a huff and as soon as Erica was assured her daughter wasn't within earshot, she turned back to Kieran. "I happen to know Stormy doesn't have enough money to pay for your services."

"Actually, she gave me all her allowance."

A meager allowance her child must have been saving for quite some time. "What was that? Fifty dollars?"

He fished in his pocket and pulled out a few bills. "Eighty, to be exact."

She rolled her eyes. "I suspect you make that much in half an hour."

"Normally, but I'm willing to give her a cut rate. In fact, you can have this back now." He opened her hand and laid the bills in her palm, then folded her fingers around them before releasing his grasp on her wrist. "In case she needs something special. Just don't let her know I returned it."

His simple touch threw Erica for a loop, almost enough to prevent her from speaking. "Why would you even consider doing this for free?"

"Because she seems like a good kid and this means a lot to her. You might want to think about that before you turn down the offer."

He definitely had a point, although Erica wasn't inclined to accept charity in any form. Yet she saw no harm in at least carefully considering the gesture before she told her daughter how much she appreciated her concern, but why she couldn't commit to a fitness program right now. "Do you have a number I can call if I decide I want to do this?"

After he pulled a card from his jeans' pocket, he gave her a long once-over that made her want to unbind her waist-length hair from the back of her neck, but that would only conceal her upper torso. "Give me a pen and I'll write down my cell number," he said. "It's easier to reach me that way."

She had no pockets in her tattered sweats, which meant she could leave him standing on the porch while she searched for a pen, or be courteous and invite him inside. Oh, what the heck. She'd write down the number and send him on his way.

Erica flattened herself against the door and waved him forward. "Come in while I find something to write with. The den's to your right."

Despite a solid effort to keep her eyes centered on his back, her gaze took a downward trek as she followed him through the small foyer. As predicted, his butt could only be deemed delicious. She seriously needed to get a grip.

In the den, Erica sidestepped over to the corner desk to prevent Kieran from getting a gander at her hips that had widened considerably since Jeff's death. That extra width was a direct result of taking comfort from food to ease the sadness, and admittedly some latent anger over being left alone to raise her daughter. She'd basically remained in emotional limbo for almost six years, even if that wasn't exactly logical. But neither was her fascination with the beautiful stranger who wandered around the room while she squirreled away the money in the desk drawer and rummaged for a pen, without success. No doubt her offspring had pilfered the last one.

"Mom! I need your help!"

Speaking of offspring… "I'll be with you shortly, Stormy." She sent a sheepish glance at Kieran, who'd paused his pacing to stand near the sofa. "When she wants something, she only knows one tone of voice—loud." Like he hadn't noticed that.

He sent her a curious look. "Is that how she came by her name?"

She leaned back against the desk and folded her arms across her midriff. "Actually, we were under a thunderstorm warning in Oklahoma the night she was born."

"Mom, if you don't come help me, I'm going to throw my math book out the window!"

"Hold your horses, Stormy! And bring me a pen." She shrugged. "As it turned out, the name fits her well."

A few moments later, Stormy walked into the room from the hall, her lopsided ponytail swaying back and forth like a pendulum. After smiling again at Kieran, she strode up to Erica and pointed a pencil at her. "Now can I get some help with my math?"

"I can try, Stormy, but I have trouble balancing a checkbook." She did know enough, though, to realize her finances were rather slim these days.

"I'm pretty good at math," Kieran said.

Stormy glanced back at Kieran, her eyes wide with wonder. "You are?"

"Believe it or not, I was an honor student in high school," he said. "I was also a business major in college. I know math. Give me a shot and I'll prove—"

"That you've got brains to go along with the brawn?" Erica blurted without thought.

He grinned. "Something like that."

"My homework's in the kitchen," Stormy tossed out before skipping into the hallway. Apparently she had no qualms about taking Kieran on as a tutor.

Erica offered Kieran the pencil and an apologetic look. "You really don't have to do this."

"Not a problem," he said as he jotted down his number on the card with the pencil and laid both on the desk.

"You don't have any pressing issues awaiting you?" Like pressing his killer body against some willing woman.

"I have to meet my parents for dinner in about an hour, so I have some extra time."

This man was much too good to be true. "What about your wife?"

"No significant other right now," he said, seemingly undisturbed by her semi-interrogation.

Very interesting information, and somewhat problematic for Erica. If he'd been involved in a serious relationship, she could easily ignore him. Absurd. She could still ignore him. "If you insist on helping my child, I won't complain. It will save me a lot of grief, but you'll probably receive some in return."

"I'm tough enough to handle a ten-year-old. And like I said, she seems like a good kid."

We'll see about that after the homework process, she

wanted to say but instead led him into the kitchen where Stormy sat behind the small dinette table, rapping her pencil impatiently on her open book.

Erica tried not to stare when Kieran shrugged off his jacket and draped it over the back of the chair that he then turned around and straddled. She tried not to ogle his prominent biceps. Tried not to gawk at the size of his hands, which he rested casually on the table before him. To say he met her expectations would be wrong. He more than exceeded them. What she wouldn't give to get her paws on all that incredible muscle mass. Professionally speaking, of course.

Jerking herself back into hostess mode, she said, "Since you don't drink coffee, is there anything else I can get you?" She'd offer him a brownie, but she'd already eaten the last one of the batch she'd made two nights ago.

He scooted the chair closer to the table. "I'm fine."

She wouldn't argue that point. "Just let me know if you need anything. I'll be right over here." Engaging in busywork while sending covert glances his way.

Erica absently swiped at the countertops with a damp cloth while Kieran went over a few problems with Stormy. Amazingly, her daughter hadn't issued one complaint. On the contrary, she actually remained silent and listened for a change.

After wiping her hands on a dish towel, Erica turned and said, "You missed your calling, Kieran. You should have been a teacher."

He looked up from the book and trained his dark eyes on hers. "No thanks. I'm better with weights."

"And I'm finished," Stormy said, then sat back and sighed. "If Mom would've helped me, we would've been sitting here until midnight."

Erica playfully slapped Stormy's arm with the towel and

then checked the clock on the wall. "Time to wash up for dinner since the pizza should be here any minute. But first, you need to thank Mr. O'Brien."

"Thanks, Kieran," she said, as if she had the right to call him by his given name.

He pushed back from the table and stood. "No problem, Stormy. Good luck on the quiz."

"I'm sure I can pass it now," Stormy replied with clear confidence, topped off with a look of gratitude aimed at her new hero. "I'll let you know how I did when I come with Mom to the gym."

Unable to voice a response, at least not one that her daughter would care to hear, Erica ushered Kieran back into the den and once there, he paused at the shelves beside the fireplace to study a framed photo taken during her gymnast days. A picture depicting a much, much thinner version of herself. "That was my senior year in high school," she said, feeling somewhat self-conscious. "I competed for a year in college before I got pregnant with Stormy."

He turned his attention from the photo to her. "You were young when you had her."

"Barely twenty," she said. And ill-prepared for Stormy's congenital heart defect, the reason she and Jeff had moved to Houston—to be closer to her doctors. She briefly wondered if Stormy had mentioned the condition to Kieran, then decided she probably hadn't. Out of respect for her daughter, who wanted badly to be viewed as perfectly normal, she wouldn't mention it, either. "I married the summer after I graduated high school, in case you're like most people and believe the baby came before the nuptials."

"My sister married young and she wasn't pregnant, either," he said. "Unfortunately, her marriage didn't last long."

"Mine didn't, either." Through no fault of her own. "My husband died in an industrial accident when Stormy was four."

"She mentioned that," Kieran said as he glanced at the picture of Jeff set out not too far away. "I'm sorry."

So was Erica. Sorry that she'd had so little time to know her husband. Sorry that her daughter had had even less time to know her father. "Sometimes things happen we can't control."

He streaked a hand over the back of his neck. "Guess you're right, but it's still got to be tough to deal with."

Erica decided to move past the sad subject. "Anyway, I intended to teach gymnastics after college. Circumstances forced me to find a more lucrative way to make a living, which is how I ended up as a massage therapist." A decision she had made in the two-year delay in receiving Jeff's employer's minimal settlement, most of which had gone to pay off Stormy's astronomical medical bills that weren't covered after Jeff's death.

Kieran replaced the photo and said, "Can you still do back flips?"

Erica smiled in response to his winning grin. "Only if I want to hurt something vital."

"After I'm done with you, you'll be able to tumble again."

She only planned to tumble into bed—alone—as she did every night. "Don't count on me doing even a simple cart-wheel."

"Then you're going to go through with the training?"

Oh, he was good. "I didn't say that."

"But you haven't ruled it out yet."

"Not yet. Obviously I haven't been able to lose the extra pounds on my own. And believe me, I've gained more than a few extra pounds." As if he hadn't noticed that in spite of her loose clothing.

"Some weight gain is understandable," he said. "You're not sixteen anymore. Body weight increases with age."

Her body had expanded more than she'd thought possible, and on a five-foot, two-inch frame, it wasn't pretty. "That's true, but come to think of it, I doubt a few training sessions will make all that much of a difference."

"A couple hours a day, five days a week, will get noticeable results."

She did a quick mental calculation. "You'd have to be darn good to whip me into shape in five sessions."

"That's for an entire month, which means at least twenty sessions. And I am good." He said it with all the assurance of a man who had no qualms about selling his skills, and not necessarily those limited to the fitness field. "But a lot will depend on your commitment after we're finished working together. I'd be willing to throw in a six-month membership at one of my clubs."

Erica would rather drink salt doused with vinegar than walk into a room full of nubile young women. "I'm not overly fond of gyms these days."

"The sessions will have to take place at the gym." He took a quick glance around the small den. "Unless you have your own equipment around here somewhere."

She had a stationary bicycle gathering dust in the garage, but that was the extent of her equipment. "No, I don't. But I really hate the thought of working out with a bunch of people looking on."

"That's not a problem," he said. "I have my own fully equipped, private area that I'd be glad to let you use until you're more comfortable."

"How convenient." Both for him and all the other women he'd probably enticed into an intimate workout. Erica could just imagine it now—a few free weights, a few minutes on the rowing machine, a lot of cardio under the supervision of a guy who probably had the means to send a heart rate to maximum level in minimal time. The vision bouncing around in her head gave a whole new meaning to the term *push-ups*.

Shaking the unwelcome fantasy away, she said, "I'm still not ready to agree to this."

Oddly, he looked almost disappointed. "Suit yourself, but you're missing a prime opportunity. I don't make this offer to just anyone."

"You're doing it for my child, remember?"

"Yeah, but I see potential in you." He raked his gaze down her body again—slowly. "A lot of potential, if you have the guts to see this through."

The challenge in his sexy voice and seductive eyes made her want to twitch and throw herself at him like some crazed hormonal harpy.

Erica led him out of the den and strode to the door, holding it open before she agreed for all the wrong reasons. "Tell you what. I'll let you know in a few days."

"Don't take too long," he said as he stepped onto the porch. "I've got a business to run and my time is in demand."

She just bet it was.

Erica felt a brush against her ankle and looked down to find the family cat winding his way through her legs. She bent, picked up the gray tabby and held him like a baby. "I was wondering where you were, Diner."

Kieran frowned. "Diner?"

"We found him behind a diner where we stopped for lunch on our way back from a trip to Oklahoma. He was scrawny and underfed, so we brought him with us, took him to the vet and got his mind off the girls."

"You had him neutered."

"Yes. Amazing how a simple procedure can improve a male attitude."

He looked pained. "Do you apply that practice with all men?"

She laughed. "Only alley cats, so don't worry."

"That's good to know. Otherwise, I might rescind the offer." He stepped off the porch and began to back down the walkway. "I expect to have an answer in two days."

A demanding kind of guy, which might have ticked Erica off if he hadn't smiled again. "Fine. I'll call you in two days."

"You do that."

While Erica remained planted firmly on the porch, Kieran turned and strolled to the sleek black sports car parked at the curb. She couldn't make out the model in the dark, but she presumed it probably cost as much as her modest three-bedroom house. And although she should go back inside, she waited until he was safely seated behind the wheel and well on his way down the street.

As tempting as Kieran's proposal might be—as tempting as he was—she didn't need any one-on-one program to help her lose weight. She could buy a DVD and some hand weights. She'd take a daily walk to get reacquainted with endorphins. She'd stop eating to fill the void.

But tonight, before she crawled into her vacant bed, Erica planned to treat herself to several slices of pizza. At least that would take care of one craving.

Chapter Two

"I need to ask a favor, dear."

Just when Kieran had claimed a spot on his sister's sofa to let his mother's Armenian cooking adequately digest, he'd been called into action by the tiny woman with a big heart. Normally he never refused Lucine O'Brien anything, but he could think of one thing in particular he wouldn't do for anyone, not even his mother. "If you want me to call Kevin and tell him he needs to be at lunch Sunday, forget it, Mom."

She wiped her hands on her apron and perched beside him on the cushion's edge. "I wish you two got along better."

Here it came, the blood-is-thicker-than-water speech. "The problem I have with Kevin has to do with his bad choices, and he's chosen not to come around. I can't change him, and neither can you." After spending most of his life cleaning up his twin brother's messes, Kieran had given up on that lost cause several years ago.

"Could you just hear me out, honey?"

Driven by family loyalty, he reached for the remote and muted the TV. "Okay, I'm listening."

She shifted slightly to face him and folded her hands in her lap. "I'm worried about Kevin. I don't think he's well."

Nothing new there. Kevin had been born the sickly twin and their mother still worried about him incessantly, even after thirty-plus years. "Why do you think that?"

"He seems tired to me," Lucy said. "And pale."

"He's tired because it's a big job, traveling all around the country to interview sports figures." And having a woman in every port, Kieran thought. Probably every airport, too.

She laid a hand on his arm. "I'd still like you to visit him and see for yourself."

That wasn't something Kieran had the time, or the desire, to do. "Let Mallory check on him."

"Did I hear someone mention my name?"

Kieran glanced back to find his sister strolling into the den, a rag sporting the remnants of strained carrots thrown over one shoulder. "Damn, you have good ears, Mallory."

"Watch your language, young man."

His mother's tone alone had been known to instill fear in many a tough guy, including his four brothers and her own husband, who was snoring like a power drill in the nearby lounger. "Sorry," Kieran muttered like a reprimanded twelve-year-old, not a thirty-four-year-old man.

"I was asking your brother to see about Kevin," Lucy said. "He somehow believes you should have that responsibility."

Mallory perched on the sofa's arm. "Whit and I had dinner with Kevin a couple of months ago, as a matter of fact, so it's your turn."

Kieran couldn't quell his suspicions—justifiable suspicions. "I'm guessing he did something that required reinforcements."

"Actually, he wanted us to meet his new girlfriend," Mallory said.

"The pro cheerleader?" The same cheerleader Kevin had used as a replacement for his former fiancée, Kieran surmised.

His father snorted loud enough to rouse the neighborhood hounds. "Nothing wrong a'tall with a cheerleader. They tend to be a limber lot."

When Kieran and Mallory laughed, Lucy brought out the visual guns again and aimed them on their father. "Go back to sleep, Dermot O'Brien, before I make you walk home." She turned her attention to Mallory. "Is she a nice girl, dear?"

"She's very nice and she's *not* a cheerleader."

"Are you sure she wasn't hiding her pom-poms?" Dermot chimed in, earning him another frown from his wife, and a grin from his kids.

"Actually, she's a pediatric resident," Mallory said. "Whit thinks the relationship has potential, but I believe the jury's still out."

His sister, always the attorney. "She's definitely not Kevin's typical girlfriend," Kieran said.

"With the exception of Corri," Mallory added.

"And look how he treated her." Although Kieran had tried to temper his tone, the ever-present animosity filtered out. But he still hadn't forgiven his twin's careless disregard for a genuinely nice woman.

"That worked out for the best," Lucy said. "Otherwise, Corri would never have married your brother Aidan."

And Kieran had tolerated enough Kevin talk to last a lifetime. Leaning over, he picked up his empty glass from the coffee table and without another word, set out for the kitchen, Mallory trailing behind him.

"You should give Kevin another chance," his sister said,

as he set the glass in the sink. "I think you'll find he's changed."

Kieran leaned back against the counter. "Because he's dating a woman who can put two sentences together before applying more lipstick?"

"Because Aidan and Corri have forgiven him, and so should you."

That was news to him. "What he did to Corri was only one episode in a long line of screwups."

"Nobody's perfect, Kieran. Seems to me you should stop and consider that, otherwise you're never going to have a long-term relationship."

Must be "grill Kieran night." "In case you've forgotten, I've had a couple of long-term relationships, including one that ended a few months ago."

"Almost a year ago, and exactly what happened with that relationship, dear brother?"

"It just wasn't—"

"Perfect?"

Damn, she was majorly annoying him. "We weren't compatible. She liked opera, I liked baseball. She liked Thai food, I prefer good old American beef. End of story."

Mallory sent him a serious scowl. "She was also extremely beautiful and built like a fashion doll. Have you ever been attracted to anyone who wasn't the epitome of physical perfection?"

Erica Stevens briefly flashed in his mind, catching him off guard. He had to remember she was a client—a prospective client—and off-limits. Regardless, he had to admit she was attractive in a wholesome kind of way. And if she decided to accept his offer, he'd have to ignore that attraction. "I don't know what point you're trying to make, Mallory, but I wish you'd make it so I can go home."

"My point is, you're too rigid, too quick to judge. You live your life by a set of strict rules—"

"What's wrong with that?"

She held up her hand to silence him. "Life isn't perfect, Kieran. People aren't perfect. You should try to relax, open your mind to all the possibilities. Being more spontaneous couldn't hurt, either."

At least now he had some ammunition. "As a matter of fact, I did something spontaneous today. I agreed to provide personal training to a woman, free of charge."

Mallory gave him a cynical smile. "She must be exceptionally gorgeous."

"She's a widowed mom, and I really didn't pay that much attention to her. We just met a couple of hours ago, at the request of her daughter."

She laid a hand against her throat. "Mr. Macho didn't notice a woman? She must be in her golden years."

"She's thirty," he said, surprised by his defensive tone. "And if you're that damn curious, she has long red hair, light blue eyes. She's short, but then she's also a former gymnast. She has great dimples. One's more prominent than the other. I couldn't tell much about her body because she was wearing baggy clothes, but from what I could see, I'd guess—" He halted his assessment when Mallory chuckled. "What's so funny?"

She laughed again. "You. I could've sworn you said you didn't notice her, and you're describing her in more detail than my husband would probably describe me."

Kieran hated to admit she was right, so he wouldn't. "Where is Whit, anyway?" he asked, only then realizing his brother-in-law had been missing since the last of the O'Brien siblings and their significant others had left for home.

"He's changing the twins' diapers in the nursery," she said.

"And just a word of advice, Kieran. When you're helping this woman with her fitness regime, you might want to look beyond the superficial. You might find that the old adage about skin-deep beauty is true. If you keep an open mind, she could be the perfect girl for you."

Time to set his sibling straight. "First of all, I don't get involved with clients. And secondly, she hasn't agreed to the training sessions yet."

Smiling, Mallory pulled the rag from her shoulder, tossed it aside and checked her watch. "Sorry to end this conversation, but the girls will be hollering for their bedtime feeding and Whit can't help with that."

Thank God for babies with an aversion to bottles. "Fine. I'll see you later."

Mallory started away but paused to face him again. "Before I go, let me add that I'm confident you'll find a way to convince your new client… What's her name?"

"Erica."

"You'll have Erica engaged in a strenuous workout in record time."

Kieran had serious doubts about that, even though he couldn't claim a lack of disappointment if she did turn him down, for reasons he didn't care to explore. "Take my word for it. If Erica decides to get with the program, it won't be because of me."

"Are you still awake, Mom?"

At the sound of her daughter's voice, Erica bolted upright and snapped on the lamp to find Stormy standing in the bedroom doorway. As her eyes adjusted to the light, she studied her child while fighting an edge of panic. Thankfully she didn't see any indication that Stormy was in distress. No ashen cast to her round face. No blue tinge to her lips. No labored breathing. In fact, she looked precious in her pink satin pajamas with the rag-tag brown stuffed dog named Pokie clutched in her arms. But still Erica asked, "What's wrong?", a typical reaction resulting from all the nights something had been wrong.

Stormy frowned, as she'd been prone to do lately when she felt her mother was being too protective. "I'm okay, Mom. I just can't sleep."

Erica started to remind Stormy it was a school night and encourage her to try harder, but she recognized that in a scant few years, her daughter's reliance on her would begin to fade more and more, as it should. In the meantime, she would cherish these moments when she could still chase away her daughter's concerns. While they were still everything to each other, before boys and best friends claimed most of her baby's time.

On that consideration, Erica scooted over and patted the space beside her. "Climb in."

Stormy bounded across the room and jumped onto the bed, her strawberry-blond curls bouncing. A beautiful bundle of exuberance despite what she'd endured in her short lifetime—both numerous surgeries and the loss of her father.

After Stormy settled in, Erica draped an arm around her thin shoulder and pulled her close. "Did you have a bad dream, sweetie?"

Stormy shook her head. "I was just thinking about Daddy."

Erica's heart took a little tumble at her child's wistful tone, and she wondered if Kieran helping Stormy with her homework had somehow prompted those memories. "I'm sure Daddy's thinking about you, too."

"From heaven," Stormy said. "Do you think Daddy's an angel, like Grandma says he is?"

Erica dearly wanted to believe in angels, but over the past few years, Jeff's presence had begun to fade, even though she still resided in the house they'd leased when they'd moved to Houston to be closer to Stormy's doctors. "If Grandma says it's so, then it's probably so."

Stormy pulled the blanket to her chin as if she intended to stay awhile. "Tell me *the* story, Mom."

Erica didn't have to ask which story she meant; she'd recited it often enough. "You mean the night you were born?"

Stormy grinned and nodded.

Even though she wanted to go back to sleep to prepare for the busy day ahead, Erica didn't have the heart to tell her child it was much too late for telling stories. Instead, she tapped her chin and pretended to think. "Let's see. Best I recall, it was a typical Oklahoma spring. We were under a severe thunderstorm warning and—"

"That's where I got my name," Stormy added.

Erica sent her a mock scowl. "Do you want to tell it?"

"I was a baby, Mom," she said with a sigh. "I don't remember that night."

Erica remembered every precious—and precarious— moment. "Anyway, I thought you might be born at home because it took your dad forever to find that baseball glove he'd bought you."

"Because he thought I was going to be a boy."

This time Erica decided not to scold her over the interruption. "That's right. But the minute you were born, he took one look at you and fell in love." She still remembered the awe in Jeff's eyes the moment Stormy came into the world, followed by the fear.

Stormy smiled again. "And when he heard me cry, he said I was going to be a country music singer."

That cry had come much later, one little detail Erica had chosen not to share with her daughter. She also hadn't told her how close she and Jeff had come to losing their precious baby, whose heart had begun to fail only hours after her birth, leading to the first of four corrective surgeries. "He said you were either going to sing or umpire baseball games."

Stormy hesitated a minute before asking, "Do you still have that baseball glove somewhere?"

Only one of the many keepsakes Erica had clung to in order to preserve the memories. "It's in the cedar chest. Why?"

"Because I'm going to need it."

"Show and tell?"

Stormy rolled her eyes. "We haven't done that since first grade. I'm going to need it because Lisa wants me to play softball with her next spring. We're supposed to sign up in January."

Serious concerns came crashing down on Erica. "First of all, the glove's too small. Secondly, you've never played softball before. Are you sure you're up to it?"

Stormy stiffened, looking determined. "I can run fast and I can throw harder than a lot of boys. My P.E. teacher says I'm a natural athlete."

If that happened to be true, Stormy had come by it genetically. Aside from Erica's gymnastics acumen, Jeff had been a talented football player. Yet for years her daughter had been held back by her physical deficits. She had no right to hold her back now, but still… "Before you sign up for anything, we need to check with Dr. Millwood. You can ask him when you have your appointment in February."

"They'll pick the teams before then, Mom." Stormy unconsciously touched the top of the vertical scar peeking out from the parting in her pajama top. "Besides, he told me the last time I saw him that I could do anything I was big enough to do, and I'm big enough, and well enough, to play softball. I can practice with Lisa. It'll give me something to do while you're training with Kieran."

The time had come to let her daughter down easy, at least on one front. "I promise I'll consider the softball issue, sweetie. But I don't think the training is going to work for me right now."

"You aren't going to do it?" Stormy said, both her tone and expression reflecting her displeasure.

"Maybe later." Or never. "But I really love that you wanted to do this for me."

Stormy pulled her legs to her chest, rested her chin on her knees and gave her a mournful look. "Daddy would've wanted you to stay in shape. He would've wanted me to play softball."

A masterful manipulation if Erica had ever heard one, even if Stormy happened to be right. Nothing would have pleased Jeff more than to see his daughter excel at sports and his wife maintain a healthy lifestyle, and her weight. "I realize that, but I don't want you to get hurt if you're not ready for sports."

Stormy climbed out of the bed and propped her hands on her hips. "Just because you're afraid doesn't mean I have to be afraid."

"I'm not afraid. I'm only concerned for your well-being, Stormy."

"You are too afraid!" Stormy stomped her foot, something she had never done before. "Lisa says you're paranoid, and she's right. You're afraid I'm going to get hurt and you're afraid to let Kieran train you because you're afraid of guys. You're afraid of everything, Mom. And I'm afraid I'm going to be stuck in this house with you until I'm too old to have any fun."

With that, Stormy spun around and headed down the hall, her hair wagging with a vengeance against her back.

On the verge of tears, Erica leaned back against the head-board and released a broken breath that bordered on a sob.

In some ways, Stormy was right—she was afraid. Her daughter would never know how many nights she'd stayed awake and watched each breath she took, fearful it could be her last. How afraid she'd been when she'd received the call informing her that her husband would never be coming home. That fear had admittedly driven her to be too overprotective, but she couldn't stomach the thought of something happening to her baby girl, the most important person in her life.

One thing she did know—Stormy had been wrong about her fear of Kieran. She wasn't afraid of him at all. She was afraid of how he made her feel in the short time she'd been around him. Afraid of acknowledging that she was highly attracted to a man, as if she was somehow being unfaithful to Jeff.

Still, she couldn't imagine Kieran would persist if she didn't go through with the training. At least she hoped not. She'd had enough trouble explaining her reasons for refusing to her daughter. She couldn't battle them both.

"Stormy's here, and someone else is here to see you, girl-friend."

Erica stopped restocking the therapy room and took a quick glance at the clock before depressing the intercom on the wall. "My next appointment's not due for another half hour, Megan."

"He's not here for a massage. He says he's the dancing pizza man. Do you want me to call the cops?"

Erica's heart did a little skip-beat rumba over the thought of seeing Kieran O'Brien again. Apparently an impatient Kieran O'Brien since less than twenty-four hours had passed since he made the offer. Oh, well. She might as well tell him face-to-face no thanks to the training, and be done with it. "Law enforcement isn't necessary. I'll come downstairs to meet him."

And down the stairs Erica went, practically sprinting. She slowed her steps when she reached the second landing because she certainly didn't want him to believe she was excited to see him. Yet when she paused at the bottom of the staircase and caught sight of him entering the salon area, she could barely catch a normal breath. She certainly wasn't the only one who'd noticed him.

From the stylists' stations lining both sides of the lengthy aisle, clients and beauticians alike snapped their heads around, risking whiplash. And those who didn't simply studied him in the mirrors' reflections, including Mrs. Weldon, a seventy-something Houston icon who'd come in for her weekly shampoo and style. Several mouths dropped open, and the once-boisterous conversations quieted to a low murmur, although Erica wouldn't be surprised to hear a round of catcalls.

She couldn't blame them one bit. Who wouldn't notice a good-looking, well-built guy wearing a fairly fitted T-shirt that showcased his perfect torso and loose black workout pants that concealed what she could only assume were a pair of unbelievably toned legs and thighs? The unruly hair and eternally shadowed jaw only added to the perfect physical package. All he needed was a sword to complete the pirate persona.

Arms dangling at his sides, he continued forward without hesitation, with all the confidence of a man who possessed the catalyst that could bring a woman to her knees in worship—undeniable masculine beauty. He kept his dark eyes leveled on hers, causing Erica to clasp the front of her white coat closed to cover what he would definitely find lacking in her body.

When he reached her, Erica managed a weak smile. "What a nice surprise, Mr. Pizza Man. Are you here for a cut and style, or are you just checking the place out?"

"I came specifically to see you." He glanced over his shoulder before regarding her again. "Can we go someplace more private where we can talk?"

This sounded like serious business, spurring Erica's curiosity. If luck prevailed, he was taking back the offer, relieving her of the responsibility of declining. And for some reason, that filled her with a touch of regret. "We can go upstairs. I need to get the bed ready." Would someone please save her from the Freudian faux pas? "I meant I need to prepare the room for my next client."

He rewarded her with a grin. "I knew what you meant."

She waved a hand toward the staircase. "Right this way."

Erica would have preferred to follow behind him, but since he had no idea where he was going, she had no choice but to lead the way and hope he wasn't totally turned off by her derriere. After they reached the top floor, she navigated the mazelike hallway while chatting incessantly about the various therapies going on behind closed doors, from European facials to peppermint body wraps.

After drawing a breath, she paused at the place that housed the wet area. "We have his-and-hers saunas, but the owner only installed one whirlpool. I'm hoping she eventually adds another to allow for segregating the genders."

"I don't see anything wrong with men and women hanging out in the same hot tub," he said, the first words he'd uttered since she'd begun the tour.

Spoken like a guy. "Some women would prefer not to mingle with men while in their swimsuits." She would be one of them.

"You have a point."

She also had an appointment in less than twenty minutes, and that sent her to the end of the corridor. "This is my domain," she said as she opened the door.

Kieran followed her inside, and while she stood at the head of the narrow bed, he walked around the room, investigating all the trappings that came with the job. After a time, he turned and leaned back against the bureau. "You know how to set the mood."

"Excuse me?"

He took another visual jaunt around the area. "Soft music, candlelight, massage oil. A lot of bare flesh."

"Middle-aged executives with hairy backs."

His smile arrived, but only halfway, with full effect. "Now you've gone and ruined it for me."

She moved to the opposite side of the room, putting the bed between them. "It's not that kind of a massage parlor, Kieran. It's therapy, although I will do a Swedish massage if someone prefers more relaxation than rehabilitation."

"You mean if they're wimps."

She pulled a set of sheets from the cabinet behind her before facing him again. "Some people would prefer not to have their pressure points manipulated."

He moved closer to the bed. "I don't mind a good manipulation of my pressure points now and then."

If he was like most men, he had one particular pressure point in mind. Not that she was totally averse to the prospect. "I'd be glad to give you a good *therapeutic* massage." And hoped she survived it. "Just stop at the front desk on your way out and make an appointment."

"You can't work me in today?"

"I have a client coming in shortly, remember?"

"Define *shortly*."

She took another quick glance at the clock. "Fifteen minutes or so."

"What can you do for me in fifteen minutes?"

Surely he wasn't serious. "I'd barely get past your neck."

"Some other time then." He planted his palms firmly on the bed's unmade surface. "I'd definitely want my back done."

She smiled. "Is it hairy?"

"No. Want to check it out?"

Boy, did she ever. "I trust you. Now please tell me why you're really here." Other than to make her relatively large work space seem very small, especially when he leaned over and propped his folded arms on the table while angling his body away.

"I thought I'd plead my case about the benefits of physical fitness," he said.

So much for him withdrawing his services. "I know all the benefits, but I also know that my time is at a premium these days."

"Did you stop to consider how much your daughter wants you to do this?"

"She mentioned that to me last night." Under no uncertain terms.

"She's the one who convinced me to try again with you."

Apparently her daughter had borrowed someone's cell phone. "I'm sorry she called and bothered you."

"She didn't call. She came to the gym again this afternoon with the Conrads and asked me if I could give her a ride over here."

That was worse than a phone call. "She did what?"

He straightened and raised his hands as if to ward her off. "Before you decide to march into the waiting room and ground her, you need to hear me out."

A grounding was definitely in Stormy's future, but she agreed to hear him out first. "I'm listening."

"Stormy's worried about your health and your happiness. She honestly thinks that a fitness program will help you with both, and she's right. You can't fault her for wanting what's best for you."

No, Erica couldn't. In fact, she was deeply touched by her child's concerns, even if she didn't care for Stormy's persistence. "I understand why she's worried, but I'm still not sure I can go through with this."

"Yes, you can, with my help. In a month's time, you'll wonder why you waited so long to get with the program."

In a way, she recognized he was probably right and almost voiced that when the sound of a shrill ring interrupted both her thoughts and the conversation.

After Kieran tugged the cell from his pocket and flipped it open, he muttered a harsh, "Yeah."

Trying not to eavesdrop, Erica straightened a few things on the shelf as Kieran spoke to the party on the other line. But she couldn't ignore the bitterness in his tone when he said, "I don't have time for this right now."

When Erica faced him again, Kieran remained silent, the tension almost palpable. His current problems, whatever they might be, definitely superceded Erica's decision. "If you need to take care of business, Kieran, we can talk about this later."

He pocketed the cell and said, "Not business—my brother. Kevin believes his schedule is more important than mine when he wants something. And he *always* wants something."

Granted, Erica didn't have a great relationship with her own brother, but that stemmed from a substantial age difference and general apathy. "Do I detect some sibling hostility?"

"We're twins, and let's just say I'm tired of taking the flak for his mistakes."

"Identical twins?" Erica had a hard time believing that another version of this stunning guy walked the streets of Houston.

"Yeah. People have always had trouble telling us apart. Especially women."

"I could see where that might be a problem, particularly with a woman involved."

"And that's happened more than once," he said. "A few

years ago, I was in a bar and a woman came up and slapped me. It took me an hour's worth of explanation and buying her two drinks before she finally believed I wasn't the one who slept with her, then dumped her."

Erica sensed a solid case of good twin, evil twin. "He's really that bad?"

"He's spoiled. My mother catered to him because when we were born, she almost lost him. And since then, he's always been perfect in her eyes." The hint of resentment in his tone was unmistakable. "Sorry. I didn't mean to go off on that."

"I understand it completely. There's nothing like that bond between mother and child." Even at the ripe old age of twenty, Erica had realized that the first time she'd held her newborn daughter. And she could definitely relate to almost losing a baby. "Speaking of kids, I need to get a move on, otherwise I'm going to stay behind all afternoon. That means getting Stormy home late."

He surveyed her face from forehead to chin before centering his gaze on her eyes. "You haven't given me an answer yet."

That's because she didn't have one, although she was heading toward the affirmative. "I'm still concerned about working it into my schedule."

"I've come up with a plan that should help with that. I can come to your place for a jog in the morning to take care of the cardio, then you can come to the gym in the evening for strength training."

He was definitely being accommodating, something Erica couldn't help but appreciate. "That might work. I'll think about it and let you know by tomorrow."

He rounded the table and stood by her side. "Don't give yourself more time to obsess over it, Erica. Say you're going to do it right now. You'd don't have to be afraid of it."

You're afraid of everything, Mom.

Erica tried to discard her daughter's indictment, without success. As a few moments of nagging indecision passed, she hugged the bedding closer to her chest while Kieran continued to stare at her, assessing her, dissecting her.

"Okay. I'll do it," she said, before she had time to make more excuses.

Kieran didn't look the least bit surprised. But then, he'd probably known all along he'd eventually wear her down. "Good. Tomorrow morning, I'll be at your place at 7:00 a.m. In the meantime, have your doctor fax me a consent form stating you're healthy enough to start the program. The fax number's on the card I gave you. Do you still have it?"

She felt the urge to salute, or to drop the sheets from a sudden desire to explore all his prime bulk with her hands. Fortunately, she did neither. "Yes, I have the card, but I told you I'm not a morning person."

"And I told you if you try it, you'll like it. Besides, tomorrow's Saturday."

His determination was second only to Stormy's. "I still have to be at work by ten, and I need to wash and dry my hair, which takes a while. Could we wait and begin on Monday? That would give me more time to get used to the idea."

"The longer you put it off, the more time you have to change your mind," he said. "I'll be over at six instead of seven and we can do some preliminary prep before we go for a run. That should give you ample time to get ready for work."

Lovely. A crack-of-dawn jog didn't sound at all inviting to an out-of-shape, thirty-year-old woman. "What kind of preliminary prep are you referring to? Aside from the usual stretching."

"I have a form for you to fill out about your overall health and I'm going to take your measurements and calculate your body fat. I'll weigh you tomorrow at the gym."

Erica's mouth dropped open momentarily before she said, "That's like saying you're going to read my diary."

He had the nerve to grin. "Do you have a diary?"

As a matter of fact, she did. A very private journal that she kept hidden away in her lingerie drawer. "That's none of your business, and neither are my measurements." A hot flush flowed over her cheeks when she realized how ridiculous that sounded.

Now he appeared frustrated. "Look, unless we have a starting point, we won't know how much progress you've made. And if you're worried what I'm going to think, believe me, I know a lot of women who'd kill for your body."

Oh, sure. "How would you know? You haven't really seen it."

"Trust me, I know." His gaze wandered to her breasts for a split second before he returned his attention to her eyes. "Some things you can't hide, even with baggy clothes. You have to learn to embrace your body type because no one has a perfect body. You only need to drop a few pounds and do some toning."

He might change his mind about that once he wrapped a tape measure around her hips. "All right. You can take my measurements, as long as you promise not to stare." Or laugh.

He raised one hand in oath. "I promise I'll be totally professional."

"Fine. Now I have to finish readying the room. And since you've detained me, you can help me make the bed."

He returned to the opposite side of the table and favored her with another blatantly sexy smile. "Not a problem. I'm good with sheets."

He was likely good between the sheets, and that was a place Erica didn't dare go with Kieran, even if the thought had crossed her mind.

The desire that had been dormant for years sprung to life—

followed by the usual measure of guilt. The same guilt she'd experienced when she'd considered dating in the past. Yet she couldn't help but believe that meeting Kieran O'Brien could be the springboard she needed to move forward into a future that didn't revolve solely around work and her child. That alone gave her some serious resolve.

Not only would she do this for Stormy, she was going to do it for herself.

After all, how hard could it be?

Chapter Three

Crawling out of bed before dew covered the lawn was as bad as forgetting to buy coffee, which Erica had, and that only encouraged her bout of irritability. On top of everything else, she'd barely finished dressing, brushing her teeth, washing her face and fashioning her hair into a misshapen ponytail before the doorbell rang.

Erica muttered a few choice oaths on her way to answer the summons, most aimed at Kieran's early arrival. Yet before she opened the door, she plastered on a fake smile that slowly withered with one look at him.

With his dark, longish, slightly damp hair and buff body, he could easily be mistaken for a gladiator, regardless of the clipboard clutched in his hand and absent loin cloth. She briefly wondered what he might look like in a loin cloth while resisting the urge to take a downward visual excursion. Instead, she kept her attention fixed midchest on his hooded navy sweatshirt. Even in standard workout apparel, he could put most men to shame, while she resembled something Diner might drag in from the Dumpster.

When he said, "Mornin'," Erica found him to be much too chipper for the crack of dawn—correction—*sliver* of dawn since the skies showed only limited light.

"You're ten minutes early." Her tone sounded unmistakably prickly, from lack of both sleep and caffeine.

He checked his watch and had the gall to grin. "Guess I am. Want me to wait in my car until six?"

Not such a bad idea at that, but one she couldn't in good conscience consider. After all, he was accommodating her schedule, not his, even if he had shown up at an obscene hour. "Not necessary. Come on in."

She held the door open wide while he passed by her, bringing with him a burst of cool air and a noticeably clean scent. Not that she intended to notice anything about him, but her intentions ran amok when she followed behind him and realized he was wearing shorts—to-the-knee shorts—that offered her a fine glimpse of his equally fine calves.

"Are you nuts?" she asked once they entered the den.

His frown indicated he thought she might be. "Excuse me?"

She waved a hand toward his legs. Bare, muscular, enticing, hairy legs. "You're not wearing pants."

Kieran looked down as if he didn't have a clue what he was wearing. "I prefer to run in shorts. Is there a problem with that?"

Erica could think of one big problem—her wandering eyeballs. "Seems to me it's a bit cold to go outside half-dressed."

"It's almost fifty degrees right now, and the highs are going to reach seventy today."

So much for the first seasonal cold front. "That's what I love about Texas, frigid one day, sweltering the next. Makes me miss the Oklahoma ice storms."

"You really aren't a morning person, are you?"

She felt a tad bit ashamed of her attitude. "Unfortunately, no. But by noon, I'm a really nice person."

"Since I won't be here at noon, I'll take your word for it." He offered her the clipboard. "I received the form from your doctor, but I still need you to fill out this medical history. It's only a few general questions."

A few hundred health questions, Erica realized when she took it from him and perused the text. "Looks like our first jog will have to wait if you expect me to answer all of these."

"It won't take that long if you hurry."

"I'll try, but remember, I'm barely coherent."

Erica took a seat on the sofa while Kieran claimed the well-worn brown suede lounge chair across from her. Jeff's favorite chair—just one more thing she hadn't had the heart to discard.

Getting back to the business at hand, she answered no to almost all of the queries about her physical condition, then stopped short when she came to the part about her weight. "I'm not sure how much I weigh."

"Leave it blank. Like I said, I'm going to weigh you this evening and we'll fill it in then. Since you've got to be at work, I've decided to wait and do the rest of the assessment at the club."

Meaning he'd handed her a short reprieve from having her measurements taken and her body fat calculated. Even so, she'd still rather eat dirt. "Fine."

Going back to the forms, she answered the intimate questions with serious trepidation, read the complex waiver and signed on the dotted line before handing it back to him. "Now that you know my *extremely* personal history, what's next?"

He set the forms on the table, slapped his hands on his thighs and stood. "We're going to start off easy. Just a short jog to the park up the street and back."

Erica could already feel her muscles begin to protest. "The park up the street is at least five blocks away. How am I supposed to manage that?"

He grinned again. "Put one foot in front of the other and propel yourself forward."

Oh, what she wouldn't give for a snappy comeback, or the courage to kiss that smirk off his pretty face. "Very funny. I believe you said we're starting out slowly. Running five blocks and back doesn't qualify as 'slow' in my opinion."

He inclined his head and gave her a challenging look. "If you can't handle it, I guess we could walk."

She shot to her feet, answering his dare. "I can handle it. I used to run at least two miles a day when I was in gymnastics training." Training she'd undergone practically back when dinosaurs were in diapers.

He gestured toward the foyer. "Then let's get going so you can wash your hair."

The man had a mind like a steel trap and a body that served as bait for any woman halfway interested. She wasn't interested, at least not that much. "First, I have to check on Stormy."

Leaving Kieran behind, she walked to her daughter's room and quietly opened the door. With her blond hair fanned out over the lavender satin pillow case, Stormy slept soundly on her back, arms sprawled wide, one leg jutting from beneath the covers as if prepared for a hasty escape. Funny, Erica had once slept in that same position, until Jeff's death. These days she spent most nights curled on her side, hugging her pillow, an inadequate replacement for someone warm to hold.

Erica started to wake Stormy and let her know she was leaving, but reconsidered. Once her daughter learned that Kieran had arrived, the child would no doubt be out of bed in a flash, delaying their departure. The quicker she got this first phase of the taskmaster's program over, the better.

After closing the bedroom door, Erica made her way back to the den to find Kieran still waiting, still looking much too sexy for such an early hour. Obviously he was an early riser, and that unearthed an image she had no business imagining.

After a brief mental scolding, she immediately strode to the desk, disengaged her cell phone from the charger and grabbed her keys.

"Are you expecting a call?" Kieran asked when she turned to face him.

"I always take my phone everywhere I go, in case Stormy needs me."

"She probably won't even realize you're gone before we get back."

"Probably not, but I'll feel better knowing she can call if she needs something. It's bad enough I have to leave her alone in the house."

He sent her a curious look. "She doesn't stay by herself?"

"Rarely, and only for a half hour or so on weekends, while I'm running errands during the day."

"What do you do with her while you're working?"

"If she's not at work with me, she stays with Mrs. Carpenter next door or at a friend's house."

She sensed what he was thinking—Erica's paranoia runs rampant—particularly when he followed her to the door and she armed the security system with the standard code—a code that signified her and Jeff's wedding anniversary.

"Glad to see you're adequately protecting yourself," he said before adding, "although this is a virtually crime-free neighborhood."

She stepped onto the porch and double-checked the lock. "There isn't any such thing as a crime-free neighborhood these days." After pocketing her phone and keys, she turned to him again. "You never know when some strange man's going to appear at your doorstep, intent on torturing you."

His smile made the torture worthwhile. "Do you remember how to stretch?"

She tried not to be too insulted. "Yes, I remember." Which was no guarantee that she might not tear something in the process.

Erica followed Kieran's lead as he went through the motions of warming up his muscles. She also followed the line of his leg, from the top of his cross trainers to the bend of his knee and the curve of his thigh. For some reason, she kept right on going to a very male area no decent mother should dare go—

"What equipment do you prefer?"

Her gaze snapped to his as a heated blush slapped her cheeks. "Beg your pardon?"

His grin deepened, indicating he'd noticed her wicked perusal. "Maybe I should ask what event you preferred during your gymnastic days."

Thank heavens that's what he'd meant. "I did fairly well with the beam, bars and vault, but floor exercise was my forte."

"And that involves quite a bit of running, right?"

"Yes, that's part of it."

"Good. Then let's go."

When he took off down the walkway toward the street, Erica realized the moment of truth had arrived. Would she make it two blocks without collapsing? Of course she would—she hoped.

When Erica passed by his black sports car parked at the curb, she discovered it happened to be a Porsche. Figured. He looked like a Porsche kind of guy. But she didn't have time to admire the dream vehicle if she wanted to catch up with him, which she did in short order since he'd maintained an easy jog, not a full-out sprint. Despite her calves' and ankles' slight protests, she managed to keep up with his pace...until he sped up, leaving her behind. After a few yards, he turned and ran in place. "You can do better than that."

If she had the energy, she'd take off her aged sneaker and hurl it at him. "I'm coming," she said around her labored breathing. "Feel free to go ahead without me."

"No way. I don't want you heading back home."

Going back home sounded like a good plan, but she'd be darned if she'd give up now, so she continued on regardless that the occasional patch of grass began to resemble a nice place to take a nap.

By the time they reached the park, Erica's feet stung and her lungs burned. She managed to make it to a nearby play yard where she used a support beam to hold her up while she caught her breath.

Kieran looked no worse for the wear, or winded in the least, and that brought about a return of her foul mood. "Are you trying to kill me our first day together?" she managed around a few puffs of air.

"Not at all," he said. "By next week, I'll have you jogging to the park and back, plus a couple of laps around it."

By next week, she might be bedridden with several stress fractures. "I hope you know CPR." Another pleasant fantasy filtered into her mind—Kieran's mouth covering hers. Short of feigning respiratory arrest, it wasn't going to happen.

"That's a requirement that comes with the job, but you're not going to need it." He pulled the sweatshirt over his head, leaving him clad in only a white T-shirt that rode up momentarily, giving Erica a glimpse of the dip of his navel and the happy path running beneath it.

If he kept that up, she'd definitely need some serious resuscitation. "Thanks for the vote of confidence. Let's just hope I can live up to your expectations."

"You already have." He draped the sweatshirt over the side of the slide, stepped closer and braced two fingers on Erica's neck.

"Looking for something?" she asked.

"I'm checking your heart rate."

Of course he was, and how stupid for her to think anything else. "Am I still alive?" Her rapid heartbeat indicated she was quite alive—a partial reaction to his touch, no matter how innocent—or clinical—it might be.

He dropped his hand from her neck, much to Erica's disappointment. "Yeah, you're still alive. We'll work on getting your rate up a little higher in the future."

Any higher and she might suffer a cardiac arrest to go along with her shin splints. "If you say so."

"Are you recovered enough to head back now?"

From the run, yes. From his hand on her neck and his close proximity, not exactly. After a couple of deep knee bends that caused her moderate pain, she shook out her shoulders and lifted her chin. "I'm ready, and even if I wasn't, I need to get back to my daughter."

Kieran studied her for a long moment before saying, "She's lucky to have you as her mother."

"And I'm blessed beyond belief to have such a great daughter. She's the best thing that ever happened to me, and I'd do anything for her."

"The answer is no, Stormy. End of discussion."

"But, Mom, you're not being fair!"

Kieran stood in the den, listening to the verbal volley between mother and daughter coming from the kitchen. It wasn't his place to dive into the fray, and so far he'd avoided any intervention. In order for that to remain true, he needed to make a quick departure to allow the familial fireworks to calm. But before he could head out, Stormy rushed into the den and aimed a puppy-dog look on him, halting his escape.

"Isn't she being unfair, Kieran? I mean, what's wrong with playing softball?"

So much for remaining out of the battle. And so much for pretending he hadn't overheard the conversation. "Your mom didn't say you couldn't play softball. She said she didn't see any reason to buy equipment before you signed up. I'm sure as soon as you're on a team, she'll buy you all the equipment you need."

Erica entered the room with a calm facade, but Kieran could tell by the flash of frustration in her blue eyes she wasn't too pleased with her kid, or with him. "That's right, Stormy. I don't see the need to go out and buy a lot of softball gear before we've decided you can play."

Stormy braced both hands on her hips. "Before *you* decided if I can play, you mean. I've already decided I want to play. And just because you wear old clothes doesn't mean I have to wear old clothes. When I go to the mall today, I want to get some stuff so I can practice."

Erica gave a solid tug on her sweatshirt and frowned. "First of all, I didn't say you could go to the mall. Second, I'd rather be with you when you buy your clothes."

Stormy looked as if she was ready to reload until a horn sounded, sending her straight to the window. After peeking through the blinds, she spun around again. "They're here, Mom. They've come all this way to pick me up. We're going to play at Lisa's, then go to the big mall, the one with the skating rink. *Please* let me go."

Erica blew out a frustrated breath. "All right, you can go. But I don't have any cash on hand to give you right now."

Stormy scowled. "Lisa's mom lets her use her credit card."

"No way," Erica said. "You're too young to use a credit card."

"But I need new sneakers, Mom. At least let me buy those."

Kieran wouldn't be surprised if Erica yelled, but instead she added in an even tone, "We'll buy you new sneakers as soon as I get paid next week."

Erica sounded self-conscious, probably over being forced to drop her pride and admit to him that her finances weren't all that solid. In an effort to keep the peace, Kieran pulled out his wallet, withdrew a hundred-dollar bill and offered it to Erica, possibly at his own peril. "Take this for the time being."

"I can't let you do that, Kieran," Erica said. "Stormy can wait a week."

Stormy, on the other hand, ignored her mother, snatched the bill and smiled. "Thanks, Kieran. I'll pay you back with my Christmas money."

"I'll work it out with your mom." Kieran repocketed his wallet and regarded Erica. "Consider it an advance for the massage you're going to give me next week."

Her eyes went wide. "You booked an appointment?"

"Not yet, but I will."

The ringing doorbell halted all conversation. "I'll get it," Stormy called as she sprinted down the hall.

"Tell Candy to come in and give me some details," Erica called back.

Kieran bit back a curse. "Candy as in Candice Conrad?"

"The one and only," Erica answered.

Although confirmation wasn't necessary when he heard, "You girls wait in the car while I speak with Erica."

Hell, this was all he needed—the last thing he needed. He'd spent several months avoiding Candice as much as possible. Sneaking out the back door seemed like a damn good plan, although he might have to explain to Erica why he didn't want to be in the same room with the woman.

Candice whisked into the den on a cloud of expensive perfume and an air of supremacy, wearing too-tight jeans and a cleavage-revealing sweater, not a blond hair out of place. "Hello, Erica. Stormy said you wanted to talk to—" Her words died in her open mouth when her gaze fell on Kieran. "What a surprise. I wasn't expecting to see you here, Kieran."

"He's my personal trainer," Erica said, before Kieran had enough presence of mind to respond.

Candice raised a perfectly manicured hand to her throat. "I see. I didn't realize you could afford Kieran's services."

"We have a deal," Kieran said without thought. "I oversee her fitness program, she gives me massages in exchange."

Kieran wasn't sure which of the two women looked more shocked.

Erica cleared her throat. "What time do you think you'll be through, Candy?"

"I'll drop Stormy off here after dinner, around seven."

"We'll be at the club," Kieran said, before Erica had a chance to answer, or change her mind. "You can drop Stormy off there."

Candice's expression brightened. "Not a problem. I'll come prepared to work out. Maybe you can give me a few pointers on the new elliptical?"

Lighten up on the mascara was the only pointer he cared to give her, unlike Erica, who wore next to nothing on her eyes and looked damn good regardless. "I'll be busy. Joe or Evie can help you."

She didn't bother to mask her disappointment. "I suppose that will have to do, at least for tonight. I'll find a time to pin you down later."

He sure as hell didn't want her to pin him down in any shape or form. "Have fun shopping, Candice." He had no doubt she'd greatly enjoy spending her husband's fortune.

"We'll have a marvelous time, as always." She flipped a hand in Erica's direction. "And don't worry, Erica. I'll make sure the girls stay with me."

"Thank you," Erica said. "You know how I worry when they're in a crowd."

"Yes, I know. You've reminded me every time I take them out." With that, Candice turned on her spiked leopard-print heels and strode out of the room.

"Don't go anywhere," Erica said to Kieran as she backed toward the hallway. "We have a few things to discuss after I tell my daughter goodbye."

Kieran started to remind her that she still needed to get ready for work but reconsidered. He figured his immediate future held a good chewing out, and he might as well take it like a man.

A few minutes later, Erica returned to the den sporting a serious expression. Assuming this could take a while, Kieran dropped down onto the sofa and waited for the lecture.

Erica stood in the middle of the room, arms crossed over her midsection while she nailed him with a hard stare. "Don't get me wrong. I do appreciate your generosity, and I realize you've probably always had money to toss around on a whim." Her tone indicated she didn't appreciate it one damn bit. "However," she continued, "I can provide for Stormy, even if it doesn't seem that way to you. Therefore I'd prefer you not undermine my authority with my child."

Time for Kieran to set her straight. "I'm sorry for overstepping my bounds, but you're dead wrong about one thing. I haven't always had money. I grew up less than two miles from here in your average, middle-class neighborhood. My father's a retired postal worker, my mom stayed at home to raise her kids. They worked hard for a living and I've worked equally hard for every damned dime I've ever made."

Her features softened somewhat. "I just thought that—"

"I was born with a set of sterling silver weights in my hands?" He came to his feet, battling his own anger. "Not even close. I wore my brothers' hand-me-downs until I was old enough to get a job and buy my own clothes. I also learned early on what it's like to be around the Candice Conrads of the world. If I hadn't given Stormy the money, Candice might have taken it upon herself to buy the shoes just to feed her own superiority by making you feel like you can't give Stormy what she needs."

She raised her hands, palms forward, before dropping them to her sides. "Okay, I understand what you're saying." She studied him for a long moment. "I may be making another wrong assumption, but it doesn't sound like you care too much for Candy."

A definite understatement. "She's not my favorite person."

"But didn't you used to be her personal trainer?"

"Yeah, for a few months. It didn't work out."

She crossed her arms once more. "Let me guess. She didn't like you telling her what to do."

According to Candice Conrad, no one told her what to do to any extreme, something he'd discovered five minutes into their first training session. "We had different goals. I wanted to get her into shape, she wanted to get me into bed." And that was way too much information to hand to Erica, someone who had a social relationship with his former client. Normally he'd never be that open with a current client, but something about her made him want to confess his sins.

"Did either of you reach your goals?" she asked.

"Not even close." And not for Candice's lack of trying. "I'm sorry for being blunt. I forgot she's your friend."

She released a caustic laugh. "She isn't my friend. She's Stormy's friend's mother, and that's the extent of our relationship. I appreciate the fact that she's willing to watch Stormy while I'm at work, but we're not close enough to have afternoon tea or go out for happy hour together. We don't run in the same circles, and that's fine by me."

He found Erica's attitude very welcome. Many of the women he'd trained before cared more about scaling the social ladder than mastering the stair climber. "She doesn't strike me as the kind who'd get along with many women."

"Or men," she added. "Stormy told me yesterday that she's getting divorced."

That was news to Kieran, not that he cared aside from the fact that it would only feed her determination to worm her way back into his life. "Great. Now she can live happily ever after with her husband's money."

They shared in a laugh before Erica checked the clock on the wall. "It's getting late. I need to—"

"Wash your hair." He smiled and she smiled back. "I'll get out of your hair then, pun intended. But first, one more question." One that had piqued his curiosity as well as his concern. "Why are you so set against Stormy playing sports?"

"It's complicated," she said as her gaze wandered away.

He roosted on the arm of the sofa. "I'm a fairly smart guy, so I can do complicated."

Kieran could tell Erica wasn't too keen on explaining, but after a few seconds she said, "Stormy was born with a heart defect. She's had four corrective surgeries in the past ten years."

Damn. He hadn't expected that. "Why didn't you tell me sooner?"

"Because Stormy doesn't want anyone to know she's anything but normal, so please don't mention it to her."

He could certainly understand why a child would feel that way, but he couldn't fathom why someone as nice as Erica Stevens had had more than her share of problems. It damn sure wasn't fair, not that life always was. "What's Stormy's health status now?"

"According to her doctor, she's cleared for normal activity," she said. "This is the first year she's participated full-time in P.E. since she started school."

"If that's the case, sounds to me like softball would fall into that category."

"Yes, that's probably right. But I still worry about her." The concern in her tone made that very apparent to Kieran.

He came to his feet again. "Look, softball is one of the safer sports as long as the proper equipment is used. My sister played for years and never suffered more than a few scrapes from sliding into second base. And I can help Stormy practice, maybe play some catch with her to see how she does."

"I'm sure you're much too busy to worry about that."

In a way, she was right. But for some reason, he felt he had to do this for her daughter, especially now that he knew what she'd been through. "I can schedule some time for her. I could pick her up from school, take her to the batting cages and then meet you at the club."

She sighed. "Kieran, I honestly do appreciate it, but I can't afford to pay you anything right now. I still owe you for the sneakers."

"You can pay me with a massage."

Her eyes widened. "You're serious about that?"

Oh, yeah. "I told you yesterday I could use a good one. Is a hundred dollars for an hour of your time about right?"

"That's what I charge, but that's not what I make. The spa takes forty percent of my earnings as commission."

That royally sucked for her. Something occurred to Kieran—an alternative plan that would save them both time. "You wouldn't have to pay the commission if we didn't do it at the spa, correct?"

She frowned. "Where do you propose we do it?"

"I have a place at the club you can use. Just bring your oil and your candles and your magic hands."

"You mean we'll do it under the table?" Her smile and dimples came out of hiding. "No pun intended."

"Under the table, on the table, it doesn't matter to me."

The innuendo suspended the conversation for a few seconds before Kieran turned the topic back to business, something he should've never strayed from in the first place. "Meet me at the club around six-thirty tonight and be prepared to work your butt off. We'll work out the massage details sometime next week."

She braced her hands on the back of the chair, her cheeks slightly red from the blush that he'd obviously put there. "That's my plan, to work my butt off. Literally."

Kieran's plan entailed keeping his hands to himself unless it involved personal fitness, not personal pleasure. He worried those plans could go awry.

No denying it—something about Erica had him not only wanting to confess his sins, but wanting to engage in a few with her. Maybe it was her sense of humor, her vulnerability. Her killer red hair, innocent dimples and big blue eyes. Maybe it was more about her concern for her daughter's health, the burden she'd borne since the loss of her husband. Whatever the reason, he couldn't deny the attraction was stronger than it should be.

After ten years as a personal trainer, Kieran O'Brien could count on one hand the female clients that had interested him enough to forget his code of ethics—one. Erica Stevens. And he'd be damned if he let that happen.

Chapter Four

Erica had endured stalled traffic due to two fender benders, construction on the freeway and crazy drivers with aversions to blinkers just to get to the club on time. Since her arrival in Kieran's office, she'd suffered huge calipers pinching her skin in places that shouldn't be pinched all in the name of body-fat calculation. She'd stepped on a state-of-the art digital scale…with her eyes closed. Now the real torture was about to commence—her measurements.

"Raise your arms," Kieran said as he stood behind her, close enough to create a bit of discomfort for Erica on several levels.

She quelled the urge to say something snide, like how she hadn't had so much fun since she'd had her wisdom teeth extracted. Instead, she remained still and silent while Kieran worked the measuring tape around her breasts. He only lingered briefly before going back to his desk to record the numbers on the dreaded clipboard that now held every last one of her intimate secrets. Okay, maybe not all of them. He still didn't know the size of her feet, the smallest things on her entire body.

When Kieran came back and lifted her T-shirt to measure her waist, Erica had a very conspicuous reaction—a frank covering of gooseflesh all over her body. She wondered if he'd noticed. She hoped not.

"Are you cold, Erica?"

Great. He'd noticed. She faked an innocent look over her shoulder. "Maybe a little." A lie. In reality, she was rather toasty. Both hot and cold, like a malfunctioning kitchen faucet.

"You won't be cold when you start working out," he said.

"I have no doubt about that."

Erica had no doubt that the next measurement would be the most challenging. She held her breath when she felt the tape tighten around her butt, praying it was long enough to span her hips. When she felt it release, she experienced an overwhelming sense of relief.

Kieran went back to jotting down the results and after he tossed the pen aside, looked up at her and grinned. "Now that wasn't so bad, was it?"

Easy for him to say. "Can I see the results?" As much as she dreaded seeing the information, the suspense was nearly killing her.

"Sure."

After drawing in another fortifying breath, Erica took the few steps to view the verdict. Her weight wasn't as bad as she'd thought—it was worse. And heaven help her, she'd need a tent to fit her blossoming butt if she didn't do something, and soon.

She spun around and nearly bumped into Kieran, who'd clearly been looking over her shoulder. "I want to lose thirty pounds by the first of December."

He moved to her side and leaned back against the desk. "Ten to twelve pounds would be a reasonable goal in a month's time."

"By Christmas?"

"Twenty pounds is possible, as long as you stick to a healthy diet."

Which meant the end of her favorite comfort food—brownies and ice cream. "I understand that's part of it, and I'm willing to adjust my diet."

He folded his arms across his broad chest, bringing his bulging biceps clearly into view. "I'll set you up an appointment with our staff nutritionist."

She shook her head. "Not necessary. I know what to eat and when to eat it. I was in training once upon a time, remember?"

He pushed away from the desk. "Okay, but if you change your mind, let me know. Now it's time to go to work." He pointed at the double doors on the opposite side of the glass-and-chrome-appointed office. An office that rivaled any corporate raider's workplace. "Let's go."

Erica had a difficult time getting her feet to move. "Is that where you keep the whips and chains?"

"Nope, just my own private facility. The whips are chains are upstairs in my apartment." He topped off the comment with a grin.

"You actually live here?"

"Yeah. I decided it was easier that way. No fighting the traffic any more than necessary. It's convenient, and has a great view of the city. I'll give you the grand tour at some point in time."

"You could give me the tour now." Not necessarily advisable, being alone with Kieran in his home even though she trusted he'd behave. She wasn't certain she trusted herself.

"We've done enough procrastinating already," he said, his tone slightly scolding. "Time to get with the program."

Ah, the program. The real reason she was there. "Okay, if we must."

"Don't look so worried. I'll go easy on you tonight."

Oh, sure. Like he'd gone easy on her that morning during their jog.

Kieran crossed the room and Erica hung back, enjoying the view of his confident gait, the slight swing of his arms, the breadth of his back encased in a black form-fitting T-shirt and, admittedly, his butt.

After he threw open the doors and signaled her forward, she reluctantly joined him at the opening that revealed a fitness paradise, if one appreciated the myriad equipment. Erica recognized some of the machines that resembled steel monsters ready to swallow her whole, and some she didn't. Regardless, she suspected he was going to instruct her on the use of each and every one, whether she knew how it worked or not.

And that's exactly what he did—put her through the proverbial ringer, moving from machine to machine. She pedaled, rowed, stepped and sweated with Kieran's encouragement. But somewhere between the recumbent bike and the elliptical, he morphed from consummate cheerleader into demented drill sergeant. He only paused to hand her a bottle of water that he allowed her to drink for a few seconds before demanding she continue. And if she heard "Keep going, Erica" one more time, she might have to tie him up with the jump rope hanging in the corner so she could gag him with her sock.

By the time she finished with the free weights, every bone, joint and muscle in her overworked body screamed in protest. And before he could order her onto another torture device, she collapsed and stretched out on the floor mat beneath her sore feet.

Closing her eyes against the harsh fluorescent lights above her head, she muttered, "Enough," with the last of her waning respiration. Luckily she'd seen several portable defibrillators scattered through the club, should her heart prematurely decide to throw in the towel.

When she didn't receive an immediate response, Erica forced her lids open to find Kieran hovering above her, an annoyingly sexy and somewhat devious gleam in his eyes. He wasn't done with her yet, she feared. He confirmed her concerns by saying, "While you're down there, let's do a few crunches."

Even attempting a scowl took too much energy. "Let's not."

He crouched down beside her. "Don't wimp out on me now."

At this rate he was going to put her into an endorphin coma. Since he probably wouldn't let up until she did his bidding, a compromise was in order. "I'll do ten."

"We'll see," he said with all the cockiness of a man in complete control.

She shoved her hands behind her neck and lifted her head, her face screwed up with the effort. She could only imagine how she looked at the moment—stray hairs plastered to her forehead, sweat drenching her T-shirt, fire-red cheeks as she battled her body's continued resistance.

"You're not working your abs," Kieran said.

She fell back and groaned. "I am, too."

"No, you're not." He moved to the end of the mat and held her feet down. "Now try it."

She executed one whole crunch and asked, "Satisfied?"

"Not yet." He braced one palm on her knee and rested the other on her belly. "Give me ten more."

Erica struggled to answer his command, all the while trying

to ignore the placement of his palm. A large palm lingering right below her belly button, sending all sorts of randy thoughts into her brain. Maybe crunches weren't so bad after all.

"Faster," he barked out. "Tighten those muscles. Keep your legs slightly open. Don't stop now. That's it. You're doing great. Work it, babe."

"Anybody home?"

When Kieran glanced over his shoulder, Erica braced on her elbows and raised herself up enough to see an extremely attractive, exceedingly tall, brown-haired man dressed in business casual standing between the open doors.

Kieran stood and swiped a hand over his forehead. "What's up, Aidan?"

"I had lunch with Whit today and he asked me to drop this by on my way home." He held out a rolled paper tube and offered it to Kieran. "It's the updated blueprints for the south location."

"We're almost finished," Kieran said. "If you want to wait around a minute, we can have a beer in the apartment."

"No thanks. Corri's holding dinner for me." The man leaned around Kieran and of all things, winked at Erica. "From what I heard a minute ago, I've interrupted something a hell of a lot more interesting than having a beer with your brother."

His brother? Erica dropped her head back on the mat and shut her eyes tight for at least the tenth time this evening.

"She's a client, Aidan," Kieran said. "I'm training her."

"Training her for what?"

"Shut up, Aidan."

Erica ventured a look to see the man grinning as he slapped Kieran on the back, hard. "Never mind. It's none of my business. Carry on, and take your time."

With that Aidan left, closing the doors behind him while

Kieran muttered a couple of expletives that were not nearly as shocking as his brother's assumptions. And Erica, like any self-respecting, thoroughly mortified woman in the throes of exercise stupor, sat up and did the only thing she could do—laugh.

It began as a slight chuckle before transforming into a raucous chortle. Kieran stared at her like she'd grown a second head as she held her aching sides and tried to catch her already labored breath. After a time, she finally composed herself enough to quiet down.

"Are you done now?" he asked.

She released one last chuckle, which earned her a serious glare from Kieran. "Sorry for laughing, but I found his assumptions pretty funny."

"Believe me, you wouldn't laugh if you had to endure Aidan's harassment. And take my word for it, he'll be doing plenty of harassing in front of the whole family tomorrow during Sunday dinner."

Fond memories of a better time flitted through her mind. A time when she and Jeff had joined their families for weekend meals before Stormy was born. "You have dinner with your family every Sunday?"

"Most Sundays," he said as he propped the tube against one wall before walking to the nearby weight bench. "With all the siblings and their kids crowded into the house, sometimes it's complete chaos. I like to take a break now and then."

"Exactly how many siblings do you have, aside from the three I know about?"

"All total, four brothers and one sister, all but one married with kids."

Erica couldn't begin to imagine having such a large family. "Wow. I only have one brother living large and single in Seattle, and I haven't seen him in three years."

He picked up a weight and with one hand, worked it with

ease, his biceps flexing with the effort. "What about your parents?"

"My dad's a farmer, my mother raised the kids and kept the house running smoothly. She lives to spoil my father. I don't think either of them could survive without each other." Erica didn't look forward to the day when either of them had to find out if they could, in fact, survive.

"Sounds like we have similar backgrounds."

"Guess you're right." She hugged her knees to her chest, trying hard not to stare at the continued play of Kieran's muscles. "How many nieces and nephews?"

He set the weight aside and casually draped both arms on the bar suspended over the bench. "At the moment, three nieces and three nephews, but that's subject to change at any time. My brothers have made procreation a sport."

If they looked as good as Kieran and Aidan, she doubted they had any trouble picking willing teammates. "How do you keep up with everyone?"

"I have a chart in my den. Every time someone pops out a kid, I fill it in."

She didn't even use a spreadsheet for her finances. "Really?"

He grinned. "I'm kidding. If you're around enough, it's not hard to keep up."

As much as she'd enjoyed getting to know more about Kieran's life, reality set in when she glanced at the clock on the wall. "Stormy should be here any minute."

He strode back to the mat and held out his hand. "You're finished for the night, so you can get up off the floor now."

After she allowed him to help her up, Erica kneaded the palpable knot between her shoulder and neck. "It's times like this I wish I could give myself a good massage."

"Did you pull something?"

"No, but I have a huge knot right here," she said, touching the place. "Guess I wasn't doing the crunches correctly after all."

Instead of saying I told you so, Kieran took her by the shoulders, turned her around and started rubbing the sore spot. "How's that?"

"Feels great." And it did. Really great. "You're pretty good with the massage technique, O'Brien." She flipped her pony-tail over the opposite shoulder to give him more access. "But I'm better at it."

"I'm sure you are, and I intend to find out in the near future when you give me my massage."

Erica couldn't wait, possibly at her own detriment.

While Kieran continued to work her sore muscles, thoughts of the encounter with Aidan O'Brien returned, threatening to send Erica into another fit of laughter. "You really didn't find it the least bit funny, having your brother stop by while you're chanting, 'Tighter. Work it, babe. Spread your legs'?"

He halted his massage midstroke. "I didn't say 'spread your legs.'"

She sent him a frown over her shoulder. "I could've sworn that's what you said."

"Believe me, if I'd said that, you might be flat on your back, but you wouldn't be doing crunches."

She turned to face him. "Exactly what would I be doing?"

He reached up and pushed a strand of hair away from her damp forehead. "Let's just say you'd be doing something more interesting than working your abdominals."

Erica forgot all about her stiff neck when Kieran's gaze drifted to her mouth. Forgot that he was her fitness coach and by his own admission, bent on keeping their relationship totally professional. She'd also forgotten until now what it was like to be in that defining moment right before a kiss, when everything disappeared except the need for human contact—the need to know she was still desired. Then again, perhaps she was only imagining he wanted to kiss her. As she swayed slightly forward, he framed her jaws in his hands, and right then she knew with certainty that she hadn't been imagining a thing.

When his mouth covered hers, warm and oh so welcome, Erica's arms automatically went around his neck while he settled his palms beneath her ribs. She momentarily considered the dangerous path they were taking, but decided she didn't care. Her awareness centered on how much she had missed this intimacy. How much she appreciated his undeniable skill, his gentleness that directly contrasted with his diehard training methods, the soft, seductive glide of his tongue against hers, his body melded to hers. The kiss soon turned deep, more deliberate and extremely deadly to Erica's composure.

"Mr. O'Brien, there's a little girl named Stormy looking for Ms. Stevens."

The blaring intercom startled Erica back into reality and sent Kieran away from her. She suddenly recalled the rare nights Jeff had come home early only to have their attempts at alone time thwarted by Stormy. Maybe this was a sign that what just happened, shouldn't have happened. The repentant look on Kieran's face led Erica to believe he definitely felt that way.

She hooked a thumb over her shoulder, more embarrassed than she'd been since she'd met him, and that was saying quite a bit. "Guess I should go find the kid."

He grabbed a towel from the weight bench and swiped it over his face. "Probably a good idea."

"I'll see you Monday morning."

"I'm overscheduled on Monday," he said as he tossed the towel aside. "Let's make it Tuesday evening here at the club and skip the morning run. We can add cardio to the strength training."

"Sounds fine." A chance to sleep in a bit later, yet Erica couldn't help but wonder if the kiss had something to do with the schedule adjustment. If maybe he'd decided coming to her home wasn't such a grand idea.

"About what just happened…" he said, fueling her suspicions. "I'm sorry. It won't happen again."

"No big deal," she said as she backed toward the door. But it had been a big deal. Something she would have a lot of trouble ignoring. Something she'd have to learn to ignore, because as he'd said, it wouldn't happen again. Yet she couldn't help wishing that it would.

"When's it okay to kiss a boy, Mom?"

Erica had to brake hard before she ran right through the red light. Surely her daughter hadn't witnessed the kiss she'd shared with Kieran. No way. Stormy had been waiting by the front desk when she'd sought her out at the club. "What brought that on, Stormy?"

She glanced at Stormy to see her shrug. "Me and Lisa were talking about it today at the mall. She said she's been thinking about kissing a lot and she says she's ready. So when is it okay to start kissing?"

Lovely. After her up-close encounter with Kieran's talented mouth, that was the last thing Erica needed to think about right now, especially while navigating a moving vehicle. "It depends, Stormy. Maybe when you're fourteen or fifteen." Or twenty-five, if Erica had her way.

When Erica guided the car into the subdivision, Stormy asked, "How old were you when you kissed Daddy the first time?"

Uh-oh. This could definitely come back to bite her. Jeff had been the literal boy next door, her very best friend, until the summer before junior high when they'd locked lips in the cornfield, a rite of passage for every farmer's daughter. "I was a little older than you." But not by much.

"Where did he kiss you?"

"At the farm."

"No, silly. I meant was it on the cheek or on the mouth?"

She shot through the stop sign before lifting her foot from the accelerator to prevent a citation. "On the lips."

"Was it a French kiss?"

At this rate, she was going to take out a few mailboxes before she made it the remaining two blocks to the house. "Sounds like someone else has been thinking about kissing."

"Maybe," Stormy said quietly. "I've been thinking about kissing this boy at school."

Just one more block, Erica. "Does he want to kiss you?"

"Lisa says he does."

Hold the wheel steady. "Does this boy have a name?"

"Randolph James Hillyard. We call him R.J. He lives by Lisa."

Great. Her daughter's first crush—a rich little lothario. She turned onto their block and sent a quick look Stormy's way. "Are you two going steady?"

Stormy wrinkled her nose. "Huh?"

Obviously that whole concept was passé. "Are you two a couple?"

"He's going to be at the party next Friday."

She pulled into the driveway much faster than necessary and managed to stop before plowing into the garage door. "What party?"

"Kaylee's birthday party. Don't you remember?"

No, Erica didn't, but then her mind had been wandering quite a bit lately. After putting the car in Park and turning off the ignition, she shifted to face her daughter. "This is a boy-girl party?"

Stormy rolled her eyes. "Yeah, Mom. We're too old for baby parties."

Erica didn't consider not quite eleven as too old for anything except perhaps a tricycle. "I might not remember you mentioning this party, but I do know I haven't given you permission to go."

Stormy put on the pouty face that she wore so well. "I *have* to go, Mom. Everyone in the fifth grade's going. It's not like Kaylee's parents won't be there."

Erica found little comfort in that fact considering she'd only met Kaylee's mom maybe twice. "I'll talk to her parents and then I'll let you know if you can go. Okay?"

"Okay." Stormy fell silent for a moment before she asked, "Was Daddy the first boy you kissed?"

He'd been the only boy she'd kissed until they broke up for about five minutes their senior year of high school. She'd made the mistake of going out with Bobby Frank Feldon after a football game, a boy who had fast hands and no respect for girls. After that night, she'd appreciated Jeff even more, and they never spent a moment apart again. "Yes, Daddy was the first boy I kissed."

"Do you miss kissing him?"

Until tonight, she hadn't given kissing much thought. She'd intentionally not thought about it for several years, because if she did, she'd only be inviting the familiar ache, the sense of loneliness she'd tried so hard to discount. "I'm missing my favorite TV show, so let's get into the house."

Stormy scooted out of the car while Erica retrieved her gym bag and followed her inside. She was incredibly tired, extremely hungry and somewhat bewildered. Things were moving too fast in her life, with her relationship with her child and her indisputable attraction to a man who was basically off-limits.

She wondered if Kieran had given her any thought since she'd left the club—given their kiss any thought. More than likely, he'd probably blow it off and go about his business, never to think about it again.

"That was one hot redhead you were 'working out' with, Kieran."

As predicted, Kieran would be forced to defend himself before he'd even entered the door of his parents' house. He'd already given himself a sufficient chastising for letting things get out of hand with Erica, and for reliving that kiss over and over in his mind most of the previous night.

"I told you, Aidan, she's a client. End of discussion."

"If you say so."

At least his brother had enough class to make sure no one else was standing in the driveway before he'd started hounding him. Speaking of driveways…the minute he'd pulled up, he'd noticed the place wasn't the usual parking lot. "Where is everyone?" Kieran asked as he followed Aidan up the steps to the porch.

"It's just me, you, Corri and Dad. Devin's on call and Stacy's at her parents' house with the boys," he said. "Since J.D.'s with his dad, Jenna and Logan went away for the weekend."

"Which means she'll be pregnant by tonight."

Aidan laughed. "Probably. Anyway, Kevin's—"

"Not around." Nothing new there. Kieran never expected to see his twin at family gatherings these days. "Where's Mom?"

"She went over to Mallory's to deliver chicken soup because Whit and the girls have colds, and that means we get sandwiches."

"No pot roast?" Their mother's cooking was the high point

of Kieran's week and one of the primary reasons he made an effort to be there.

"No pot roast today. But I don't care as long as the twins aren't here to expose the kid to a virus."

"Which kid?"

Aidan frowned. "My kid. Emma, in case you've forgotten."

Maybe he did need a chart. "Oh, yeah. I remember her now. Cute baby, curly blond hair, looks like her mother, thank God."

"You're damned hilarious." Aidan pulled the screen open but continued to block the entry. "By the way, Emma's asleep in our old room, so be quiet."

Kieran could handle quiet. His father, on the other hand, didn't know the meaning of the word.

He stepped inside to find Aidan's wife, Corri, seated on the sofa, a tray of sandwiches set out on the coffee table before her, and his dad, good old Dermot, fast asleep in his favorite lounger.

Corri straightened and smiled. "Hey, Kieran. Glad you could make it. We were beginning to feel like pariahs."

Aidan dropped onto the sofa and rested his hand on Corri's thigh. "I was kind of enjoying the silence for a change."

After grabbing a soda from the fridge in the kitchen and a ham sandwich from the tray, Kieran took the chair kitty-corner from the TV, focusing on the football game in an effort to ignore Aidan, who'd started nuzzling Corri's neck. He sure as hell didn't need to see overt displays of affection. He did need to finish eating, get out of there fast and go to the club to work off some excess energy while considering his current predicament—Erica Stevens. Maybe even fantasize about Erica Stevens. A little fantasy never hurt anyone, as long as he didn't go down the reality road again.

"Aidan tells me he met your girlfriend, Kieran," Corri said. "Is this the former gymnast Mallory mentioned to me a few days ago?"

If he hadn't already swallowed the bite of sandwich, he would've choked. "Yeah, she's the former gymnast. And no, she's not my girlfriend. I'm her personal trainer."

"I'm thinking you'd be a wise man to make her your girlfriend, son." Apparently his dad had been roused from his nap by his normal curiosity, as well as his penchant for making his opinions known.

"Why is that, Dad?" Aidan asked, although Kieran wished he hadn't.

Dermot released a gruff chuckle. "Because I hear gymnasts are a flexible lot."

Aidan and Corri laughed in response. Kieran didn't. Nothing about the remark was funny. Neither were the explicit images of Erica now running through his mind. Images he pushed away for the time being.

After wolfing down the sandwich and soda in record time, Kieran escaped to the kitchen to discard the trash. If he played his cards right, he could be out the door before the next round of verbal grilling.

"Leaving already, Kieran?"

Kieran glanced to his right to see his brother hovering in the doorway. So much for a fast getaway. "Yeah. I need to stop by the club before I head home."

Hands in pockets, Aidan strolled into the room. "Another floor-mat training session with the gymnast?"

A few years back, Kieran would've attempted to knock the smirk off his brother's face, even if Aidan did have three inches on him. They'd all learned how to fight by fighting each other. But he was more mature now, and throwing a punch in his mother's kitchen wasn't a banner idea. Instead, he chose a partial lie, not a fist, for his weapon of choice. "I have to do some paperwork, Aidan. That's what you deal with when you own two businesses."

Aidan leaned back against the cabinet and studied Kieran with blatant skepticism. "She's getting to you, isn't she?"

Kieran opened the pantry door and tossed the can into the recycle bin. "I don't know what the hell you're talking about." Another lie.

"You know exactly what I'm talking about. Maybe I should say *who* I'm talking about. You've got a thing for the redhead."

Kieran slammed the pantry door and whirled around. "I told you, she's a client."

"Yeah, that's what you said, but I'm not buying it. Otherwise, you wouldn't be so defensive when someone brings her up. You'd just ignore all the comments, but you're feeling too guilty to do that."

Unfortunately, Aidan happened to be right on target, even though Kieran didn't plan to admit it. "Look, she's a nice woman who wants to get into shape. She doesn't have a lot of money, so her daughter came to see me and asked me to help out. I'm doing both of them a favor without charge."

Aidan frowned. "In other words, you're providing your services for free, and there's nothing more to it?"

"Yeah." Lie number three. "Something wrong with that?"

"Not at all, except you're not telling me everything. Did things go beyond the trainer-client relationship last night after I left?"

Kieran gritted his teeth. "I didn't sleep with her, if that's what you're asking."

Aidan chuckled. "But you wanted to."

He hated that his brother read him so well. "Okay, yeah, the thought crossed my mind after I—" Nope, he wasn't going to go there.

"After you what? Kissed her?"

He didn't have the energy for another lie. "Yeah."

Aidan pointed at him. "I knew it."

"I didn't plan it. It just happened, and I'm not going to let it happen again."

"What makes you think you can stop it?"

He didn't have any choice. "Because it's unethical. Aside from the standing rules of the profession, you told me yourself that it's a bad idea to get involved with someone you have a working relationship with, even though you didn't follow your own advice with Corri."

Aidan ran a fast hand through his hair. "You're right, but it turned out okay. Better than okay. And the way I see it, you have two options. You let nature take its course and see what happens. Or you cut if off now, because even if you can bench-press a building, you're not strong enough to ignore the chemistry."

He didn't care for his brother's options or opinions. "I'm not you, Aidan, so you can kiss my—"

"Don't say it, young man."

Kieran turned to the right where his mother stood immediately inside the kitchen, holding a plastic container. Lucine O'Brien might be small in stature, but she was more than capable of carrying off the disapproving-parent demeanor in a big way. "Hey, Mom. When did you get back?"

"Just in time to hear your conversation." She set the bowl on the counter and regarded Aidan. "I believe I heard your daughter."

Aidan tilted his head slightly. "I don't hear anything."

Lucy gestured toward the living room. "Then go talk to your wife. I need to have a conversation with your brother."

That's all Kieran needed—another lecture. Only this one could be ten times as bad, depending on how much his mother had overheard. Probably more than he'd hoped, considering the stern look on her face. "This woman you're discussing," she said after Aidan departed. "Is this the widow with the child that Mallory spoke of the other night?"

Good thing his sister wasn't around. Otherwise, he'd have to give her a chunk of what was left of his mind for spinning the rumor mill out of control. "First of all, Mother, my personal life isn't anyone's business. Secondly, this whole thing has gotten blown out of proportion. I'm only supervising her fitness program."

She had the skeptic's demeanor down to a fine art. "Really? When did you add kissing to that program?"

Damn. "It was a mistake. A spur-of-the-moment thing."

She folded her arms across her middle. "Perhaps that's true, but my sons aren't inclined to do anything they don't want to do."

Lucy was right—he had wanted it. If he hadn't, that kiss would've never happened. "I don't understand why this is such a big deal. I'm going to handle it. And if you're done with the interrogation, I need to go."

"How long has she been widowed?" she asked, indicating she wasn't done.

"Six years."

"Does she have family here?"

He started to ask why Erica's life history was so important, but instead decided to answer the question and hope it was the last. "Her parents are in Oklahoma, and she has a brother in Seattle. She moved here ten years ago because her daughter was born with a heart problem."

That definitely got his mother's attention. "Is the little girl all right?"

"She's had several surgeries, but she's fully recovered."

Lucy sighed. "And that, my dear, is the 'big deal.' You have a mother who's almost completely alone and a little girl who's suffered through sickness and the death of a parent at a very young age. I would hate to think you'd take advantage of the situation, especially when it comes to a woman who could still be very vulnerable."

From the beginning, he'd recognized Erica's vulnerability when it came to her self-image, but beyond that, she was tougher than a lot of women he'd known. "I understand what you're saying, Mom, but I don't intend to take advantage of anyone."

"Of course no one intends to do that, dear. But intentions sometimes go by the wayside when a man can't—to quote your father—keep the pony in the barn."

"It's stallion in the stall, Mom." The last time Kieran suffered this much humiliation, his dad had attempted the "sex talk" using Irish proverbs. "If you're through chastising me—" and embarrassing the hell out of him "—I have to leave, Mom."

Lucy wagged a finger at him, signaling she still wasn't finished. "One more thing you should consider. You have a prime opportunity to make a positive impact on not one but two lives by being a role model to the child and a friend to the mother." She patted his cheek. "That's the road you should take, my dear. The honorable road."

His mother was right—he needed to remember the honor code his parents had drilled into him from birth, as well as the professional ethics he'd established early in his career. He would guide Erica through the fitness process, maybe help Stormy with softball and be on his best behavior, beginning tomorrow. Mondays were hell, but he'd find the time for Erica and Stormy. Besides, he'd claimed he couldn't schedule a session until Tuesday only because he'd needed to take a step back. His weakness wasn't fair to Erica, and if he was going to do this, he planned to do it right. He also planned to keep his hands—and mouth—to himself.

Chapter Five

Erica couldn't stop thinking about Kieran's mouth, no matter how hard she'd tried, and she'd tried all day long, failing regularly in her attempts.

"You're last appointment canceled, honey."

After dropping the robe onto the end of the massage table, Erica turned to face the sixtysomething salon owner standing at the treatment room door, her lips the color of hothouse tomatoes, her platinum-blond coif stiff as a springboard. "I'm sorry, Bette. What did you say?"

"Your four o'clock isn't coming, so you can go home now."

"Thanks." As bad as she needed the money, Erica wasn't all that disappointed over the no-show. Now she could take Stormy home early, go to the market and have ample time to prepare an early, healthy dinner. Afterward, they could watch a movie together. A nice, animated, G-rated movie with absolutely no kissing.

When the stylist continued to stare at her with blatant curiosity, Erica kept a tight rein on her patience for the sake of civility. "Did you need something else, Bette?"

"Just a quick question. Are you getting laid?"

The woman knew blunt like she knew big Texas hair, much to Erica's chagrin. "No, I am not getting laid. And even if I was, I wouldn't say a thing for fear the news would end up on every radio and TV station in Houston."

Undeterred, Bette strolled in and parked herself on the wingback chair across the room. "Something's wrong with you, honey. Or maybe I should say something's right with you. I've watched you all afternoon. You're distracted, and that typically means a man's involved."

Erica couldn't exactly refute that, but she wouldn't confirm it, either. "I've been busy."

"Busy, my foot, sugar. You're in la-la land. Why, you even smiled for no reason at all, even after Megan told you Mr. Winston didn't leave a tip."

Truth was, she hadn't heard Megan mention the non-tip. She hadn't heard much of anything aside from an annoying little voice in her head reminding her of Saturday night. "Okay, I'm in la-la land, but who wouldn't be? It's a gorgeous day outside."

Bette delivered an inelegant snort. "It wasn't that kind of a smile, Erica. It was a dreamy smile, like you had some guy on your mind. And I'm thinking that guy is the pizza deliveryman."

For heaven's sake. "He doesn't deliver pizza. He's a personal trainer. My personal trainer."

Bette raised a too-thin eyebrow. "What's he training you for?"

The exact same thing Kieran's brother had asked, and Erica had the same reaction—a blush to beat all blushes. "Fitness training, Bette."

"Well, if I were you, honey, I'd want more from him than a few rounds on a treadmill." Bette leaned forward and smiled. "That is, if you're interested in him."

If Erica issued a denial, she'd be handing the woman a huge fib. Instead, she opted to take the Fifth and began gathering her things.

Bette shot to her feet and pointed. "You *are* interested, aren't you?"

Erica shoved her cell phone into her bag, threw the purse strap over her shoulder and faced her interrogator. "I'm interested in getting out of here while I can still find a parking spot at the grocery store. I'll see you in the morning."

Bette positioned herself in the doorway, impeding Erica's departure. "Listen, sugar, I know I'm twice your age and I've been married to the same man since St. Peter was playing in the sandbox. But I still know a lot about the opposite sex."

"What's the point to all this, Bette?"

"The point is, you aren't getting any younger, doll. And there aren't that many cute, single guys your age, ripe for the picking." She took Erica's hands into hers, her expression surprisingly serious. "I know it was hard, losing a husband so young, but it's time you bring your life out of storage, dust it off and take it for a spin. That means going for the gusto while you still have some gusto left."

"You mean dating?"

"If you want to play it that way, yeah, dating, and all the benefits that come with the package. Your trainer man has a lot of benefits, some that can't be seen with the naked eye unless he's naked." Bette followed up with a cackle that grated on Erica's nerves like a civil defense siren.

"You're telling me that I should seduce him?" The thought of seducing any man, let alone Kieran O'Brien, seemed almost laughable.

"That's exactly what I mean, honey," Bette said as she released Erica's hands. "Remember, you don't have to marry him. But a guy like that can bring you back to the land of the living with only a little encouragement. Unless you've forgotten how to encourage. If that's the case, I can give you a few pointers. All you have to do is ask."

Erica didn't dare ask the resident gossip for advice on sex. "Thanks for the offer, Bette, but I don't have time for men in my life right now."

Bette winked. "You might just change your mind after a little more training." With that, Bette spun around and headed away with more vigor than most women her age, leaving Erica to ponder her coworker's observations.

Never in a million years would she entertain the idea of seducing Kieran. Then again, two nights ago, she didn't have to do a thing aside from engage in a little suggestive banter. That alone had earned her a kiss.

A kiss she wanted to experience again. And again. So why shouldn't she go for it? Because he'd been adamant about professionalism. Because he'd said the kiss shouldn't have happened, and it wouldn't happen again. And that was quite enough to discourage her.

Yet when Erica headed through the salon to retrieve her daughter from the break room, Bette's words echoed in her mind.

It's time to take your life out of storage…

Maybe her friend was right. Maybe she had put her life in the closet, using excuses like mothballs to preserve her memories of Jeff. Maybe it was time to move forward. And maybe Kieran O'Brien could be the cure for her inability to gain any ground.

If she had the least bit of courage, she would go for it, as Bette had suggested. She just might at that—provided Kieran didn't resign as her fitness coach, never to be seen again.

* * *

"Look, Mom! It's Kieran!"

Erica slowed the sedan to a crawl when she caught sight of a black Porsche hugging the curb in front of her house. And leaning against the hood, dressed in a tight white T-shirt that showcased his dynamite arms, and jeans that looked tailor-made, a modern-day Greek fitness god. Her first thought—why had he come to the house? Her next—she was very happy to see him. Secretly thrilled, even though she questioned his unexpected appearance, and if his resignation was imminent.

As she whipped the car into the driveway, Erica's mind zipped back to the kiss that continued to plague her, and she immediately forced the image away. She couldn't—wouldn't—think about that now, particularly with the kissing culprit on the premises.

Before Erica could get one foot out the door, Stormy jumped from the vehicle and ran to Kieran, throwing her arms around him as if she'd rediscovered her long-lost best friend.

When Stormy rushed back and announced, "He's got a surprise!" Erica calmly walked to the trunk, opened it slowly and pulled out two grocery bags in an effort to regroup before she had to face him. Yet when Kieran sauntered toward her with that same show-stopping gait, her composure dissolved like an ice cream cone on a summer sidewalk. He had all the confidence in the universe and no qualms about looking her straight in the eye, while she only wanted to look him straight in the mouth. He soon arrived where she stood like a statue, gripping the bags to her chest, as if they offered protection against all that charisma.

"Hey," he said with a smile that could easily melt the frozen foods in her grasp.

And like a fool, Erica replied, "Aren't you supposed to be at the club?" as if inconvenienced over his arrival.

He braced a hand on the top of her car, making the midsize sedan seem remarkably small. "I finished what I needed to do earlier than planned."

"So he came to see us today instead of tomorrow," Stormy added.

Erica handed her daughter the bag with the refrigerated items. "Take these in and put them away before the ice cream melts."

Amazingly Stormy skipped away without any protest, and Erica felt the need to explain her purchases to Kieran. "The ice cream's for Stormy. I bought myself frozen yogurt. Feel free to check out my receipt." *Or anything else you'd like to check out from a nonnutrition standpoint.* An absolutely ridiculous thought, concocted by a woman acting as if she were confronting her first crush.

"I didn't come here to police your food," he said.

She shifted the remaining sack to her hip. "Then why are you here?"

"To make you work so you don't lose your motivation."

When he grinned, she almost lost her grip on the groceries. "I wasn't planning on going to the club tonight, per your request. In fact, I've planned an early dinner."

"We can work out after dinner."

"Are you staying for dinner?"

"Are you inviting me?"

Erica had no problem with that, except… "Eat at your own risk. We're having fish."

"Not my favorite, but I'll eat it as long as it's not fried."

That wasn't an option according to her self-imposed diet. "I'm going to bake it."

"Sounds good to me." He pointed behind him. "I brought a few weights with me along with a few other things."

She envisioned all sorts of portable devices designed for the utmost in physical persecution. "What other things?"

His gaze drifted away momentarily. "I brought a glove and ball to play some catch with Stormy. If that's okay with you."

"Is that the surprise she mentioned?"

"Yeah."

Obviously he hadn't given the promise much thought, leaving Erica to deal with some serious fallout from her child if she refused. "If I say no, you do realize she'll be thoroughly disappointed and furious at me."

He sighed. "You're right. I guess I screwed up again."

Kieran looked so remorseful, Erica couldn't think of one good reason not to go along with his plan. "If she wants to play some catch, that's fine, as long as you're careful."

He raised a hand in oath. "I promise I'll go easy on her."

"Hopefully easier than you've been on me. My body's still suffering the effects of our *easy* workout." In more ways than one.

"Are you still sore from the other night?" he asked with concern.

"I've had a little trouble sleeping." But not from the aches and pains generated from the exercise.

"I know what you mean," he said, his somber tone contrasting with his earlier smile. "And I want to apologize again for letting things get out of hand. I'll be on my best behavior from now on. You have my word on it."

"What a shame." Good heavens, had she really said that? Before Kieran could respond, she added, "I need to put the groceries away and start dinner." She backed toward the door. "Feel free to play catch with the kid. I'll send her right out."

Erica rushed into the kitchen where she found her daughter placing the last of the dairy products in the storage bin.

"Did Kieran tell you about the surprise?" Stormy asked as

she turned and closed the refrigerator door with a twitch of her small hip.

Erica set the bag of dry goods down on the counter. "Yes, he did."

"And?"

"He brought a ball and glove so he can play some catch with you while I make dinner."

Stormy jumped up and down, her curls bouncing in time with her movement before she came to an abrupt stop. "Did you tell him yes?"

"Yes, I told him yes. Now go change your clothes and put those new shoes to good use."

After her daughter sprinted away, Erica went back to shelving the groceries and dropped two cans on the floor on her way to the pantry when her thoughts turned to Kieran. She dropped another when she heard "Did you forget something?" coming from behind her.

She glanced back to see Kieran holding the remaining two bags she'd left in the trunk. "Oh, yeah. Thanks. Put them on the counter next to the sink."

She continued to stare at the canned goods while he breezed behind her, bringing with him a slight hint of cologne that set her female radar on maximum alert. No doubt one of those expensive colognes formulated to attract women like a two-for-one shoe sale. She didn't realize until that moment how much she'd missed those masculine scents in her home. How much she'd missed having a male presence when she noticed Kieran unscrewing the lightbulb centered over the sink, the one that had burned out some time ago.

"Got another bulb?" he asked.

Fortunately, she happened to be in the right place at the right time. Unfortunately, the bulbs were on the top shelf out of her reach, and unless she put out an all-points bulletin on the step stool that had mysteriously gone missing two weeks ago, she'd have to ask for assistance. "I have some up extra bulbs in here, but I'm too short to get to them without help."

He came up behind her and stood so close that her breath hitched hard in her chest. When he reached up and took the box with ease, he brushed against her back, stealing her breath completely. Then he moved away and she muttered, "Thanks," before putting the last can and her composure back into place.

With Kieran standing in her kitchen, it would be nothing short of a miracle if she had enough presence of mind to prepare a meal. At least Stormy would keep him occupied for a while.

Kieran changed the bulb with little effort while Erica retrieved the ingredients for dinner, thankfully without flipping the snapper onto the floor. She could sense he was watching her as she pulled the bakeware from the drawer beneath the stove opposite the sink where he still stood.

"How many clients have you kissed before?" Erica blurted without thought, then ventured a quick glance behind her to gauge his reaction, only to find he didn't seem at all insulted by the question.

"Honestly?"

She turned and leaned back against the stove, casserole dish in hand. "Honesty is the best policy, as they say."

Now he looked extremely serious. "None."

She tightened her grip on the dish for fear it might end up on the tile in pieces. "Not one?"

"Nope. I've always adhered to the rules."

Unbelievable. "Why me?"

He forked a hand through his hair. "After all that laughing at my expense, it could be I was trying to shut you up."

That might have angered her had he not been smiling when he'd said it. "I guess that's one way to do it."

Kieran started to speak but instead cleared his throat. "We have company."

She leaned forward to discover Stormy sitting at the nearby dinette, tying her new sneakers. Not knowing how long she'd been there, Erica prayed her daughter hadn't overheard the conversation. That would require a very lengthy explanation.

"Are you ready, kiddo?" Kieran asked as he joined Stormy at the table.

She nodded and said, "Where's the ball and glove?"

"In my bag in the den. We can get it on our way out."

"You can go in the backyard," Erica said. "It's fenced."

He ruffled Stormy's hair. "The backyard it is. I'll meet you there."

Without a moment's hesitation, Stormy charged out the back door while Kieran temporarily left the room before returning with the ball and two gloves. She expected him to make a quick exit but instead he came back into the kitchen. "Regarding our previous discussion, I wasn't completely honest with you."

Erica stopped unwrapping the fish to listen. "Which part?"

"About shutting you up. Truth is, you're damned sexy when you're laughing and you flash those dimples. So do me a favor and don't do it again."

Sexy? She was sexy? Well how about that. "I'll try not to laugh in your presence from now on, but I make no promises."

"That's all I ask." He headed out the door, taking his incredible scent and sensual smile with him.

Erica had the urge to sing while she went about preparing the food. She also had the urge to laugh. Her spirits had definitely been buoyed by his declaration, and also by the scene taking place outside the garden window.

Stormy threw the ball to Kieran with accuracy, with more exuberance than she'd witnessed from her child before. And

Kieran softly tossed the ball back, undoubtedly making certain she wasn't injured in any way. Sheer joy showed in both their faces, and Erica experienced it, too, as well as some trepidation.

Someday in the near future, Kieran wouldn't be around to play catch, something Stormy would have to deal with. But until then, Erica wouldn't begrudge her daughter these moments, and hoped that when the time came, they could both let him go without regret.

While Erica and Stormy loaded the last of the dishes in the washer, Kieran remained at the table and watched the pair interact. He had to admit, he'd enjoyed every minute of the dinner, even if he did detest fish. But he valued the company most of all, mainly the back-and-forth banter between mother and daughter that bordered on comical at times. They didn't always agree on everything, but they were obviously devoted to each other.

As much as he'd enjoyed himself so far, he had to remember he'd come there for two reasons—to help Stormy with softball, and to fulfill his obligation to Erica by putting her through a workout, and not the workout he'd envisioned over the past two days. He wanted to blame his brother for putting the thoughts in his head, but he could only blame himself. He'd been keenly aware of his attraction to Erica from the moment he'd stepped onto her front porch. Denying that attraction wouldn't change anything. Acting on impulse would, which was why he needed to remember why he was there.

After checking his watch, Kieran realized he'd come close to overstaying his welcome. "If you two are done, it's time to get to work."

Erica came back to the table and dropped into the opposing chair. "Just give me five more minutes and I'll be ready."

Stormy took the chair next to her mother. "Can I watch you exercise, Mom?"

"No, you cannot, missy," Erica said. "But you can get ready for bed, put away your clean clothes and read the rest of the book you have to finish by Thursday."

Stormy pushed back from the table, stood and sulked toward the hallway before turning around. "Did you call Kaylee's mom about the party?"

"I haven't had time, Stormy, but I'll call her tomorrow. Now scoot."

Not only did Stormy fail to scoot, she returned to the table again, this time positioning herself next to Kieran. "Mom doesn't want me to go to the party because boys are going to be there. That's not fair, is it?"

Fair or not, he wasn't about to offer his opinion for fear of screwing up again and suffering Erica's wrath. "That's between you and your mom, kiddo."

Erica pointed toward the hall. "Go, Stormy."

Stormy blew out an exaggerated breath. "Okay. But I still don't think it's fair."

After Stormy left, Kieran couldn't help but chuckle. "She's pretty damn headstrong, isn't she?"

Erica released a humorless laugh. "You could say that. On one hand, it drives me nuts. On the other, her tenacity's gotten her through some really tough times. I just wish she'd learn a little moderation."

"Moderation is good," he said. "So was dinner."

She leaned forward, braced an elbow on the table and supported her cheek with her palm. "Was it? I thought the fish was kind of dry."

A little, but he wasn't going to say anything to hurt her feelings. "It was fine. Best fish I've had in a long time." The only fish he'd had in years.

"Do you think I'm being too protective about the party?"

He could lie and guarantee a pleasant remainder of the evening, or he could be truthful and possibly be prematurely asked to leave. "How old are the boys?"

"Mostly eleven-year-olds, I'd guess."

"Eleven-year-old boys aren't too bad. Twelve is another story altogether."

She smiled, bringing her dimples into full view. "I suppose you should know since you were one once."

"A long time ago, but I still remember some of it." Especially the memories that involved sticking up for his brother on the playground, before Kevin had finally caught up in size to everyone else his age and started fighting his own battles.

"Then you think she'd be okay if I let her go?"

He didn't particularly care for being put on the spot, but since she'd asked… "I think you should trust her to make the right decisions. She's a smart kid with a good head on her shoulders."

Erica leaned back against the chair and sighed. "But it seems so important to her to fit in. I worry that peer pressure could lead her to make the wrong decisions. On the way home from the club Saturday night, she actually asked me about kissing. She's not even eleven yet."

That could mean only one thing. "She didn't happen to see—"

"I don't think so," Erica said. "In fact, I know she didn't. Otherwise, she would've asked me point-blank why we were…" Her gaze drifted away. "You know."

Oh, yeah, he knew. He'd thought about that kiss more than once tonight. Watching Erica eat hadn't helped. She had an incredible mouth that he'd like to know much better. And if he didn't get his mind back on track, he might end up making the same mistake again. "As far as Stormy and this party goes, I understand you have her best interests at heart, but I also know from experience that if you keep the hold on her too tight, she'll rebel. My mother went through the same thing with Kevin. She was overprotective to a fault, and the backlash wasn't good."

Erica looked as stiff as a steel beam, and royally ticked off. "I believe I'm perfectly justified in my concern for her. And it's not as if I don't let her go anywhere."

"That's true, and I strongly believe in structure where kids are concerned. But Stormy's desire to play softball and attend a boy-girl party isn't the same as her asking if she can spend spring break in Cancun."

Erica rubbed both hands over her face. "Thanks for reminding me what I have to look forward to in a few years." She dropped her palms onto the table and stood. "Since I don't want to think about that now, let's move on to the suffering you're going to put me through. Otherwise, I'm going to get to bed late."

He'd prefer she not mention the word *bed*. Bed plus Erica equaled more questionable ideas. "Any suggestions on where we're going to do this?"

"In the family room," she said as she headed out of the kitchen.

He followed her down the hall, and once in the den, he took a quick look around. "We need to move the furniture back."

"Okay. You take the coffee table and I'll take the chair."

While he pushed the table closer to the sofa that rested against one wall, Erica moved behind the chair and pulled it back toward the window. She glanced over her shoulder and laughed.

"What's so funny this time?" he asked.

"I just realized that anyone driving by got an up-close-and-personal view of my butt. I hope the home-owner's association doesn't fine me for contributing to an eyesore. They have strict rules about abandoned cars, overgrown lawns, large posteriors in picture windows."

For some reason, the comment brought about Kieran's anger. "This whole self-deprecating thing you have going on about your body—you need to stop it. If you could see what I see every day at the club, people who are in a life-and-death struggle to lose massive amounts of weight, then you'd realize you have nothing to be ashamed of."

She looked sufficiently contrite. "Sorry. Old habits are hard to break."

"I know," he said, his voice much calmer than before. "And I'm sorry, too. I didn't mean to be so hard on you."

"Not a problem. Someone needs to keep me in line."

Determined to get back down to business, Kieran walked to the foyer where he'd left his equipment bag and returned to find Erica standing at the shelves, studying the photo of her husband. Aside from the deaths of his elderly grandparents over a span of several years, he'd never experienced much loss. He didn't know how she'd coped with everything she'd been through. Yeah, he did know—by keeping her sense of humor. And that only made him feel worse about his earlier outburst.

After setting the bag aside, he moved behind her and surveyed the photo she continued to hold in her grip. "Must be tough, all the reminders."

After setting the picture back in place, she turned and gave him a tentative smile. "Sometimes they provide comfort. I was just thinking about how Jeff used to tell me the same thing you just told me. I shouldn't be so hard on myself. So from this point forward, I vow to look in the mirror every morning and tell myself that I'm special. As long as I'm not naked."

Yeah, some habits were hard to break, and it could take

some time for her to break them, Kieran realized. In the meantime, he'd cut her some slack. "All kidding aside, let's get started."

"I'm game. Where do we begin?"

Kieran rifled through the bag and withdrew two hand weights. "We'll start with these. Five pounds each. Just a few curls."

Erica did as he instructed without complaining at all. She fully cooperated as he put her through several exercises, including five full-out sprints up and down the driveway, followed by the notorious crunches that had gotten them into trouble during their last session. Only this time, he used his voice, not his hands, to encourage her.

After she'd done two sets of twenty, he told her, "Stand up. I want you to do one more thing, then we're done for the night."

She came to her feet and tugged her bulky sweatshirt down over her hips. "Don't tell me. You want me to bench-press the couch."

He couldn't stop his grin. "No. I want you to put your hands on my chest and try to resist me."

She returned his smile. "Bet you say that to all the women you know."

"Just do what you're told without the commentary."

She gave him a sharp, one-handed salute. "Yes, sir."

He balled his fists against his chest. "Grab my hands, angle your body away and don't let me move."

"Oh, sure. Why don't we go outside and I'll push your Porsche around the block?"

"We'll try that next week, and next week will be here if you don't get started."

"Fine, but don't expect too much."

When she clasped his hands and delivered only a minimal push, he firmed his frame and pushed back. "Harder, Erica."

"I'm trying." And she did try, but not enough for his liking.

"Keep going," he demanded. "You're not using your legs."

Scowling, she regrouped and tried again, and he continued to prod her. "Push harder. Don't let me come forward. Not even an inch. Pretend you're fending me off because your life depends upon it."

Erica unexpectedly stopped, straightened, and before Kieran could level his next command, she planted her mouth on his. All his prior thoughts of right and wrong went by the wayside, thanks to her boldness, her man-killing lips and her unmistakable enthusiasm. She kissed him with no holds barred, adequately robbing him of any remaining scrap of free will.

He recognized he shouldn't put his arms around Erica, but he did—shouldn't actively participate, but he did that, too. If he didn't stop now, he was in danger of taking her down on the sofa where anything could happen, and most likely would. But before he tossed out all common sense, Erica abruptly ended the kiss and took a step back, her eyes wide with the surprise he was also experiencing at the moment.

He cleared his throat and rubbed a hand over the back of his neck. "What the hell was that?"

She shrugged. "I failed to resist you. Or maybe I was trying to shut you up."

"It worked."

"Yes, it did, and quite well I might add."

Damn, he didn't know whether to reprimand her or thank her. "You only have to tell me to be quiet."

"Oh. I never even considered that." She finished off the comment with a smile to beat all smiles, putting her dimples back on display.

She might not be smiling if she knew how hard it was for him not to kiss her again. How hard he was, period. "We're finished now."

She stretched her arms above her head. "Good. I'm tired."

How the hell could she be so cool after that hot kiss? "Erica, the last time this happened, I told you—"

"It wouldn't happen again." She moved in closer and patted his chest, right above his thrumming heart. "Because you don't kiss clients. Don't worry, I kissed you, so your ethics are still intact."

"That's pretty skewed logic." Even though he admittedly liked her way of thinking.

She inched a little closer, an almost predatory twinkle in her eye. "Does it bother you, having a woman make the first move?"

Did it bother him? Oh, yeah. In ways she couldn't know unless she moved completely against him, or took a look down south. "We agreed we can't do this."

"I don't recall agreeing to anything aside from the personal training, but if that's the way you want it, then you'll get no argument from me."

Kieran noted a hint of vulnerability in Erica's eyes and hated that he shared responsibility in putting it there. "At any other time, under different circumstances, if you kissed me like that, we'd be naked about now. But I'm still your trainer, you're still my client, and as long as that holds true, we both need to control ourselves."

"Fine. I have to see if Stormy's in bed."

Kieran found it amazing that she'd gone from sexy she-devil to typical-mom mode as easily as flipping a light switch. "Come to the club tomorrow at 6:00 p.m. and be prepared to work for at least two hours. We'll cover cardio and strength training then."

"Okay. I'll bring Stormy." Her smile came out of hiding again. "We probably need a chaperone."

Without responding, Kieran picked up his bag, rushed out the door and drove away before he did something stupid, like go back inside and ask her if he could stay the night. His mother's talk about honor drifted back into his brain, and as much as he wanted to make love to Erica—and he damn sure wanted that—wisdom dictated he remain strong in his convictions, or back out as her trainer and get out of her life while he still could.

He couldn't lay claim to much wisdom at the moment, because no matter how close he was to a possible train wreck, he couldn't stand the thought of not seeing Erica again.

Chapter Six

After what she'd pulled last night, Erica worried she might not have enough courage to face Kieran again. But there she was, behind the wheel and on the road to Bodies By O'Brien, preparing to confront the man responsible for some fairly suspect behavior on her part. No doubt about it, her spontaneous attempt at seduction had all the grace of a horny teenage boy on his first date. At least Kieran hadn't acted totally repulsed when she'd kissed him. In fact, he'd joined right in. And that whole naked thing was encouraging—encouraging her to work twice as hard at getting in shape. If the opportunity for lovemaking presented itself, with Kieran or with any man for that matter, she would have to...well...get naked. A prime motivator for success.

"Mom, did you call Kaylee's mother about the party?"

Erica jerked her thoughts back into the present at the same

time her face began to burn. She shouldn't be thinking naked thoughts with her daughter in the car. "As a matter of fact, I did talk to her."

"Can I go?" The excitement in Stormy's expression matched the enthusiasm in her voice.

"Yes, you can go."

Stormy slapped the console then pumped her fist. "I can't wait!"

Erica wished she could say the same for herself. Despite Kaylee's mother's assurances that the party would be constantly supervised, with nothing more shady going on than music, snacks and fruit punch, she still worried about the "boy" factor. And she'd continue to worry about it until the event was over. But right now she had another event to worry about—facing Kieran.

After pulling into the crowded parking lot, Erica claimed a space a good distance from the club's entrance and shut off the car. "Would you like to watch me today?"

Stormy looked predictably astonished. "Can I?"

"Promise you won't make fun?"

"I promise."

"What about your homework?"

"I did it at the spa." She fell silent before adding, "I love you, Mom."

Stormy's out-of-the-blue hug took Erica aback, and pleased her more than her daughter would ever know. "I love you, too, sweetie. Now let's go inside and get this over with so we can go home and have some dinner."

After retrieving her red gym bag from the trunk, mother and daughter walked hand in hand toward the club, Erica measuring her steps while Stormy practically dragged her across the lot. Once inside, she checked in with the receptionist before navigating the equipment jungle on her way to

Kieran's private fitness haven—or hell—depending on how one chose to look at it. She tried hard not to notice the thin, twentysomething women and their chic workout wardrobes, striving for perfection in bodies that were already close to perfect. Of course, not everyone happened to be flawless. Before, she'd only focused on those who put her to shame with their sculpted forms. Today, she noticed several heavier women working hard to reclaim a healthy weight. A victory of sorts.

As they neared Kieran's office, Stormy broke free and burst inside without knocking. Erica could hear her daughter conversing with Kieran, and that alone sent her heart rate into overdrive. Walking into the room and seeing Kieran wearing a white tank instead of his usual T-shirt did not help her cardiac health one bit. The fluorescent light illuminated every muscular curve, from the tips of his broad shoulders to the bulk of his biceps. And those heavenly thighs…

"Mom?"

Erica yanked her gaze from Kieran's attributes to Stormy, who looked somewhat puzzled. "What, sweetie?"

"You didn't say hi to Kieran."

Somehow her child had become the mother while she'd reverted to a teenager. A lascivious teenager at that. She sought out Kieran's face, which was a much more appropriate focal point. "How are you this evening, Kieran?"

"I'm good." He slid his hands into his pockets. "Stormy tells me you're letting her go to the party Friday night."

Erica set her bag on the chair near the door. "Yes, as long as she does her homework and chores."

"I will," Stormy said with certainty. "And while I'm at the party, you can come here to the club."

"That's not going to work," Erica said.

Kieran delivered a half smile with a full punch. "Are you going to chaperone?"

If she could get away with it without totally alienating her child, she would. "I have to drop Stormy off, plus my last massage appointment doesn't end until seven-thirty—"

"The party starts at seven, Mom. Can't you cancel your appointment?"

"No, I cannot, unless you want to get a job to pay the bills, and I don't think you're employable yet. Therefore, you'll have to be late." She regarded Kieran again. "And I'll have to work extra hard tomorrow and Thursday to make up for it."

Kieran rubbed his chin, looking thoughtful. "I won't be available on Thursday, so we'll just get a late start on Friday. I don't have anything better to do."

Erica couldn't fathom a man like Kieran O'Brien not having a Friday-night date. "Are you sure?"

"Yeah, I'm sure. You can meet me here after you take Stormy to the party."

Stormy looked up at Kieran. "Can you take me to the party, Kieran? That way I can be there on time, and you and Mom can start earlier."

"Stormy Jane Stevens, you cannot randomly ask people to be your personal chauffeur."

"It's okay," Kieran said. "I don't have a problem dropping her off." He winked. "We can go in the Porsche."

Stormy grabbed his hand and began to dance a jig. "The other kids will be so jealous!"

Erica would've loved to dissolve into the industrial-grade carpet. "Stormy, why don't you go get some juice. You can bring me back some water."

Stormy wrinkled her freckled nose. "You're going to talk about me, aren't you?"

Precisely. Erica gestured toward the door. "Go get the juice."

"Okay." Stormy dragged her feet on the way out the door, looking pitiful and put-upon.

After making certain her daughter was out of earshot, she said, "You don't have to do this, Kieran. I could arrange for someone at the spa to give her a ride."

"You need something to distract you Friday night, otherwise you'll be sitting at home, worrying about eleven-year-old boys fraternizing with your daughter."

"Gee, thanks. I'd almost put that out of my mind."

He released a low, sexy rumble of a laugh. "I'll keep you occupied so you won't have to think about it."

She could think of a few ways she'd like to be occupied by Kieran, none of which had anything to do with physical fitness, or at least not the traditional kind. "All right, if you insist. You can pick Stormy up from the spa and I'll meet you here after I'm through with my last appointment."

"Great. I'll be there at six-thirty."

"And before this is all over, I'm going to owe you a lot."

He leaned back against the wall, arms folded across his chest. "You could repay me Friday night by giving me that massage. I have a part-time P.T. who comes in to evaluate injuries. We can use her room."

The thought of Kieran lying on a table, nude, might challenge her own professionalism. But she could handle it. She *would* handle it. If need be, she'd imagine him with a hairy back. "Great. I'll bring my supplies with me."

A span of silence passed before Erica added, "And as far as last night goes, I want you to know that wasn't me at all. Must be the endorphins."

"We'll forget it about for now."

Like she could really do that. "I agree. From this point forward, we'll start over with a clean slate and pretend nothing out of the ordinary has happened."

Yet her life had been anything but ordinary since she'd met him, and she wondered if she'd ever be able to settle for ordinary again.

"How do I look, Mom?"

Erica paused from refilling the aromatherapy oil to see her daughter standing in the doorway, her strawberry-blond hair cascading in curls over her small shoulders. She wore a burgundy fitted blouse, denim skirt, black ballet slippers and…makeup?

"Stormy, what is that on your face?"

Bette stepped from behind Stormy and beamed. "It's just a little blush and lipstick, honey. Actually, colored lip gloss. Doesn't she look pretty?"

As far as Erica was concerned, she looked like an elementary school harlot. "She's ten years old, Bette, not sixteen. She shouldn't be wearing anything that remotely resembles makeup."

Stormy looked highly disgusted. "I'll be eleven in a few weeks, Mother."

"Eleven's still too young for makeup, Stormy. And what happened to the outfit we picked out last night?"

Stormy wrinkled her nose, displaying more disdain. "I didn't want to wear my old jeans, and the top's too babyish."

Too babyish? She'd bought it for her right before school started. "Where did you get this outfit?"

Stormy twirled around and grinned. "It's Lisa's. She let me borrow it."

Obviously Candice exercised no real control over her daughter's clothes. "That skirt's rather short, don't you think?"

Bette rested her hands on Stormy's shoulders. "It's barely above her knees, sugar. Besides, she has such nice legs. She should show them off."

Considering the time, Erica couldn't do a thing about the skirt, but she could manage other aspects of her daughter's current look. After rounding the table, she yanked a tissue from the holder on the bureau and offered it to Stormy. "Take off the blush. You can wear the lip gloss." Hopefully it would be gone by the time she reached the party, otherwise some prepubescent male partygoer might attempt to take it off for her.

"But, Mom—"

"Do you want to go to the party or hang out with me all night?"

Stormy grabbed the tissue and began to swipe furiously at her cheeks, then handed it back to Erica. "Are you happy now?"

She'd be happier if her daughter could stay young forever. Yet she couldn't lock her up until she turned eighteen, so she'd simply have to trust her to make wise decisions, as Kieran had pointed out. "That's much better. You still look gorgeous." And she did. If only Jeff could see their baby girl now— healthy, happy and about to attend her first coed party. Only now did she realize how quickly time had passed, the true brevity of life. How far she and Stormy had come from those days filled with sorrow and anxiety.

The intercom crackled, startling Erica back into the present. "Your six-thirty appointment's here, Erica, and so is Stormy's date. I should be so lucky, but isn't he a little old for her?"

Ignoring the receptionist's remarks, Erica depressed the intercom button and said, "Thanks, Megan. Tell Mr. Wellsly and Mr. O'Brien we'll be right down."

Before Erica could take even a step, Stormy had spun around and run out the door. Bette hooked her arm through Erica's and escorted her down the hall. "Face it, sugar. Your baby's not a baby anymore."

Erica sighed. "I know. I just don't want her growing up too fast." As if she could prevent that from happening.

When they reached the bottom of the stairs, Bette blew out a low whistle before going back to her station, while Erica paused to savor the vision across the room. Kieran had discarded his typical fitness clothes for a pair of jeans, casual boots and a beige polo covered by a black leather bomber jacket. As always, his somewhat unruly, wavy hair took the "just crawled out of bed" look to new heights. Again he earned quite a bit of notice from the last remaining patrons, although he seemed oblivious to anything but Stormy's nonstop chatter.

Erica approached the pair and Kieran greeted her with a warm smile. "Are you sure you want to turn this kid loose on all those boys?"

Just when she'd become more comfortable with the idea, he had to go and spoil it. "I'm going to ignore that comment." She fished a slip of paper from her smock pocket and handed it to him. "Here's the address to the party. It's right around the block from Candice Conrad's house."

"I know where that is," he said.

Of course he would. He'd probably been there often enough. Erica turned her attention to Stormy. "I'll have my cell phone on if you want to leave early. Otherwise, I'll pick you up a little before ten."

"Eleven," Stormy said. "That's when the party's over. And I'm going to stay until the end."

Unwilling to cause a scene, Erica replied, "Fine. Have a good time, and behave yourself."

"I will." She stared up at Kieran. "Can we go now?"

"Sure. As soon as you give your mother a proper goodbye."

Stormy left Kieran's side and threw her arms around Erica's waist. "Thanks for letting me go, Mom. And don't worry about the boys. Bette told me how to play hard to get."

The best advice Bette had doled out thus far. Advice that

Erica should follow herself. But as Kieran escorted her daughter out of the salon, with his perfect physique, blatant self-assurance and head-turning gait on exhibit for all to enjoy, Erica concluded that playing easy to get seemed much more fun.

"It's that big beige house on the right."

Kieran didn't need Stormy's direction to know he'd arrived at the right place. The circular drive in front of the semi-mansion was filled with kids crawling out of several of the finest cars new money could buy. Like he was one to talk.

His pulled the Porsche behind a blue Lexus belonging to none other than Candice Conrad. If his luck held out, he could have Stormy safely inside and be back in his car before the woman realized he'd come and gone. Apparently his luck sucked, he realized, when Candice happened to be coming out as they stepped onto the porch.

She laid a dramatic hand right above her enhanced breasts and faked shock. "Why, Kieran, I'm certainly surprised to see you."

"He brought me because my Mom's still at work," Stormy interjected, before Kieran had a chance to explain. "Where's Lisa, Mrs. Conrad?"

"Inside in the game room, waiting for you."

Stormy smiled up at Kieran. "Thanks for the ride. And be sure to keep my mom busy so she doesn't worry about me."

"You bet, kiddo," he said. "Have a good time."

"I will."

As soon as Stormy entered the house and closed the door, Candice brought out a cynical grin. "Is that part of your job now, hiring out as a private driver for the client's children? Funny, I don't recall you offering to take my daughter anywhere while we were working together."

Her daughter wasn't as good-natured as Stormy, something she came by naturally. "I'm just doing Erica a favor."

"Of course. Out of the goodness of your heart."

He'd tolerated more than enough of her sarcasm and smugness. "See you later, Candice." As little as possible, if he had his way.

But before he could take a step off the porch, she moved directly in front of him. "Did you hear I'm divorcing Everett?"

Damn. He knew exactly where this was heading—down a path he didn't intend to take. "Someone mentioned it, and I'm sorry to hear it."

She shifted the strap of her designer bag to her shoulder and smiled. "Since I'm now free to do as I please, and since you're no longer my trainer, we should have dinner together tonight. I know this nice little bistro downtown that has the best quail."

Kieran didn't find that at all appetizing, either the food or the company. "Sorry, I have plans."

Candice tapped a manicured finger against her chin. "That's right, you're supposed to keep Stormy's mother *occupied.*"

He could explain further to thwart any erroneous assumptions but opted to cut the conversation short. "That's why I need to go."

Kieran stepped off the porch and practically sprinted to the car, but before he managed to open the door, he heard, "Are you servicing Erica in ways that don't involve fitness, Kieran?"

Although he wanted to get behind the wheel and speed away, he turned around in order to set the record straight. "You really have to ask that question, knowing how I feel about the client-trainer relationship?"

"That's right. You made it quite clear you don't become personally involved with clients. But because you drove her daughter here, I thought perhaps you'd changed your mind, although for the life of me I can't believe a woman like Erica Stevens would interest you. After all, you could have your pick from a number of thin, more attractive women."

If she'd been a man, she might have found herself laid out on the pavement. "Erica's a beautiful woman, inside and out. She's also unpretentious and that's damn unusual these days. Any man would be lucky to have her."

Her hazel eyes widened. "You are sleeping with her, aren't you?"

"That doesn't deserve a response, Candice."

Without giving her one, he slid into the car and waited only long enough to make sure the drive was clear before punching the accelerator. Maybe he hadn't lied about sleeping with Erica, but he probably hadn't succeeded in masking his feelings for her, either, and that could add fuel to Candice's fire. He didn't give a damn about what she thought, but he did care about Erica, and she could suffer some repercussions due to the socialite's assumption. If that did happen, he'd have to come to her defense. In the meantime, he needed to keep a tight noose around his self-control. Otherwise, if he ran into Candice again, the next time he might be forced to lie.

"Time to weigh in, Erica."

Kieran might as well have told her to jump out of a plane at ten thousand feet with no chute. Despite the fact that she'd avoided all sweets, ate only vegetables and lean meats and put her body through the rigors of exercise every day for the past week, Erica continued to stare at the scale, looming large like some giant, evil entity, even though it was little more than a platform and a skinny pole with a box balanced on top.

"Just do it, Erica," Kieran said as he stood nearby, clipboard in hand.

"Is this absolutely necessary?"

"Yes. You'll probably be surprised by the results."

True, she could be surprised, and quite possibly disappointed. She ventured a quick glance his way before facing her nemesis again. "Do you have to watch?"

"I need to chart your progress."

"Provided I have progressed," she muttered.

"You won't know until you get on the scale."

Erica's legs had the consistency of bread dough as she stepped onto the platform. Maybe he had to look, but she didn't, the reason why she closed her eyes and waited for the verdict. And waited...

"Well?" she asked when Kieran failed to speak.

"I'd say six pounds is progress."

So certain he couldn't be telling the truth, Erica's eyes shot open as she sought confirmation—confirmation that came when she stared at the number flashing before her. "I can't believe it!"

"Believe it, and congratulations."

She wanted to shout, dance, scream and, at the very least, hug the man partially responsible for her weight loss. And that's exactly what she did—stepped off the scale and threw her arms around his neck.

When Kieran tensed, the joy over her success suddenly faded, causing Erica to break all contact. His reaction shouldn't shock her; he'd been the perfect portrait of professionalism since Monday. During their sessions Tuesday and Wednesday night, he hadn't touched her, hadn't made any suggestive comments. Of course, Stormy had been present, so he certainly hadn't kissed her. In fact, he'd barely looked at her at all. He wasn't looking at her now, either.

She strived to reclaim a calm she didn't remotely feel before she spoke again. "You're a miracle worker, O'Brien."

Finally, he met her gaze. "Don't give me all the credit. You've worked hard the past few days. You deserve it."

She also deserved an award for acting as if his rejection didn't sting like a swarm of wasps. "I still have a lot of work to do."

He crossed the room and set the clipboard on a nearby table before coming back to her. "Not to put a damper on the weight loss, but from now on, you're probably going to level off to one or two pounds a week. Maybe three."

That didn't do much to lift her spirits. "I understand that. Gradual weight loss is best. Regardless, I'm grateful for your help." She raised her hand in oath. "And I promise you will get the very best massage money can buy as payment for your expertise."

His smile lightened Erica's mood. "Are you sure you don't mind doing it tonight?"

She'd be lying if she said she did mind. In fact, she'd thought about nothing else since Kieran had left the spa an hour ago. "I don't mind a bit, but aren't we going to exercise first?" She gestured toward the rolling duffel stuffed with both massage and exercise gear. "I brought my clothes."

"We can do that afterward since you're still dressed for work."

Good point. "Okay. Lead the way."

Erica followed Kieran into the gym past the huffing and puffing patrons and into a lengthy corridor. Not far from a large break room, he stopped and opened a door that revealed a bare, padded table, a small metal cabinet with a counter and sink, and not much else.

"Will this work?" he asked.

"There's no cradle for your face, but I guess it will do." She moved inside, opened the bag and withdrew her own trusty clipboard. "Fill this out and sign it."

He took the offered forms and scowled. "Are you sure this is necessary?"

"As necessary as the forms you had me complete."

"Fine." He perched on the edge of the table, jotted down the information in record time and scribbled his signature before handing it back to her.

"No recent fevers, infections or surgeries?" she asked as she scanned his almost illegible handwriting.

He tapped his finger on the board. "It's all there. I'm the picture of perfect health."

She put the clipboard back in the bag, pulled out the towels and sheets she borrowed from the spa and then draped them over the surface. "Since this isn't a standard table, the bedding might slip so you'll have to be still."

"I'll probably be asleep ten minutes into the drill."

Erica noticed he did look a little tired, not that it detracted from his incredible looks. "Having trouble sleeping?"

"You could say that."

"Me, too."

Turning to the counter, she set out the supplies she'd brought with her and wondered whether their recent lip action had contributed to his insomnia. It certainly had contributed to hers.

Time to return to the task at hand. "After I leave the room, you can undress down to your comfort level," she said, after she faced him again.

"You mean leaving on my underwear as opposed to stripping completely?"

"Precisely."

"If I take everything off, will you be uncomfortable?"

The comment held no innuendo, only concern. "Look, Kieran, when you're on that table, you're just like any other client." At least that's how she intended to view him. "Just remember, whatever clothes you leave on could impact the effectiveness of the massage. Also remember, you'll be draped."

"I wear boxer-briefs, midthigh."

That took away all the usual guesswork. "Then if you don't want your legs done, leave them on."

"I want a full-body, so they're coming off."

At least she had been forewarned. "Okay. I'll step out of the room while you get undressed. Once you're done, stretch out on your belly and cover your lower half with the other sheet."

"I'm familiar with the massage routine," he said.

So was Erica, provided she could actually remember the technique after he took off his clothes. Of course she could. She was a therapist, well trained in objectivity when it came to the process. "Do you want therapeutic or relaxation?"

"How about a combination of both?"

"I can do that. Now let's get this started."

Without waiting for her departure, Kieran pulled his shirt over his head and tossed it aside, giving her a clear view of what she'd only imagined until that moment. He had pecs to beat all pecs, a light sprinkling of hair at his sternum and the typical six-pack. Make that a twelve-pack. Lordy, she could bounce a quarter off his abs. And if she didn't exit quickly, she might be tempted to ask if he'd let her try that.

"See you in a bit," she managed as she hurried out and practically slammed the door, using it for support until she could recover from her first good look at Kieran's body. She needed to get a solid handle on her hormones, otherwise she'd never be able to go through with this. And that was absurd. She'd massaged nice-looking, well-built men before, including a few athletes from the local universities. Granted, not once had she experienced such a strong reaction to a male physique. Then again, she didn't recall any that could hold a candle to Kieran.

Candles. Darn, she'd forgotten to bring them. Not necessarily a bad thing considering she might catch the place on fire, thank to her nerves. As far as aromatherapy was concerned, the sage lotion would have to do. Lotion that in only a few minutes, she would apply to Kieran's fantastic flesh.

She tingled all over, a totally inappropriate and unacceptable reaction. She had to don her professional persona and pretend that Kieran was any other customer, even if he wasn't. Not by a long shot.

After allowing him a sufficient amount of time to disrobe, she rapped on the door and called, "Are you ready?"

"You bet."

Before she entered, Erica rolled her neck and shook out her arms and hands, exactly as she'd done years ago during meets. Aside from gymnastics, she'd faced many other challenges in her lifetime, and had met them all. She would endeavor to do the same with the challenge waiting for her behind the closed door.

Yet all the bravado in the world couldn't keep her from growing decidedly toasty when she pushed through the door and caught sight of Kieran's clothes piled on the chair in the corner. She grew three-alarm hot when she centered her attention on Kieran stretched out the table, the gold cast to his skin contrasting with the white sheet covering his obviously bare hips. He had his head turned toward her, but his eyes were closed, a blessing since he couldn't see how flushed she was at the moment.

Slowly Erica moved to the counter, fumbling with the lotion before finally applying it to her palms. If only she could dim the lights. Since that wasn't possible, she would have to rely on her strength of will.

Like a surgeon preparing to operate, Erica turned with hands raised, ready to explore Kieran's broad back, and immediately spotted a black dragon spanning the width of his left shoulder blade. "Interesting tattoo, but I'm surprised you didn't go with those vines circling your arm."

"I couldn't hide that from my mother. She's not too keen on tattoos."

Erica found that somewhat endearing, and unanticipated. Kieran didn't fit her idea of a mama's boy. "Why did you choose a dragon?"

"It's the Celtic symbol of power. I've had it since I was eighteen. When I finally did come clean with my dad about it, he informed me it also symbolized fertility, and he personally knows all about fertility."

Erica immediately recalled her mother's claims that Mr. Collins, their neighbor and father of seven, was so fertile he only had to hang his pants on the bedpost to get his wife pregnant. She made a mental note to avoid Kieran's pants, particularly since fertility could very well run in the family. But then, making a baby with Kieran could be extremely fun... What was she thinking?

She shouldn't be thinking about anything other than getting on with the massage. Yet when a scar that ran beneath the tattoo captured her attention, she traced the jagged line with a fingertip and asked, "What happened here?"

"I fell out of a tree and caught a limb on the way down when I was twelve. It took about twenty stitches to close it up."

"Ouch." Funny, she'd expected something other than a tree-climbing accident. "I thought maybe you'd had a sports injury."

"I had one of those, too," he said. "I blew out my knee in college. I was a catcher so that pretty much ended my pro baseball aspirations."

A shattered dream. Erica could relate. "That's when you started down the personal training path?"

"Yeah, during rehab. I decided to combine the sports with therapy and use my business degree to open the clubs."

Smart. Very smart. Definitely brains to go along with all the brawn. Lots and lots of brawn.

He glanced back at her and frowned. "Are you going to actually do something other than quiz me about my tat and scars?"

Yes, Erica, do something. And that something meant she had to touch him, not eyeball him. "Sorry," she muttered as she glided her hands over the breadth of his taut back, as enthralled as a child playing with mud for the very first time. As she would with any other client, she applied moderate pressure with her thumbs along his spine and lightened her touch when she came to his rib cage. He twitched a bit, indicating he could be a little ticklish there. As much as she wanted to find out, she pulled herself back into massage-therapist mode, but not before she'd given herself a harsh mental reprimand for leaving that mode in the first place.

For several minutes, Erica concentrated on his upper and middle torso before traveling to his lower back, stopping right before skin ended and sheet began. A thin sheet that presented a tempting outline of a spectacular butt. She battled the urge to take a peek. Just a little peek.

Oh, good grief. She was behaving like a woman who'd never seen male buttocks before.

Hairy back...hairy back...hairy back...

Erica slid her hands upward and immediately found a knot between his neck and shoulder. She applied a good deal of pressure on the spot, prompting a groan from Kieran.

"Are you trying to kill me?" he asked.

She continued to knead the spot without letting up. "I'm trying to release this pressure point."

"You're trying to punish me as payback for all the pain I've caused you."

Men could be such babies. "I'm trying to help you, Kieran, just like you're trying to help me. But if it's too much for you, I'll stop."

"Go ahead. I can handle it. But I would like to relax at some point in time."

She only lingered awhile longer before she turned the technique to relaxation. "How's that feel?"

"Great," he murmured.

"Are you relaxed yet?"

"I'm getting there."

Erica had arrived at the point where she needed to change her focus. With that in mind, she folded the sheet back to expose his left leg. An incredible leg with calves that should be registered as lethal weapons. Taut, powerfully built thighs that drew Erica as strongly as her favorite mint-chocolate-chip ice cream. She went back to the counter for more lotion, seeking a moment to regroup before resuming her duty. And what a delightful duty it was, curling her hands over the hair-dusted terrain, absorbing all the details while attempting to ignore her very female response—inadvisable, unwarranted female response.

Like Kieran, she'd always been a stickler for professionalism. Granted, she knew her regulars fairly well, knew about their kids, their jobs and at times served as surrogate counselor although she rarely offered opinions. She'd always been able to manage a friendly demeanor as well as a necessary detachment, where with Kieran everything she'd learned through school and experience evaporated into oblivion. Then again, she hadn't kissed any of her regulars, either.

Determined to get through this with her wits intact, Erica rounded the table and went to work on the other leg, more objectively than she had with the first through sheer will alone. The time had arrived to work on his front side, and Erica vowed she would not allow his perfect chest to affect her. "Roll over," she said as she lifted the sheet and turned her head to one side to avoid earning even a glimpse at those intimate parts concealed by the cotton sheet.

"I can't." His voice sounded strained.

She dropped the sheet back into place. "I promise I'm not going to look."

"I mean I seriously can't turn over."

Confused over his resistance, she said, "I'm fairly sure I did nothing to paralyze you, so either you don't like what I've done so far, or you did like it and you're so relaxed you can't move."

He lifted his head again and looked back at her. "Take my word for it, I'm not relaxed. Not in the least."

Apparently she'd failed miserably in her attempts to impress him. "Am I not meeting your expectations?"

"You've exceeded them. In fact, you're too good at what you do."

"Then what's the problem?"

He crossed his arms and tipped his forehead against them. "The problem is, I can't turn over without losing a damn good deal of my dignity."

Understanding finally broke through Erica's momentary bewilderment, sending her into clinician's mode. "Don't worry. Arousal's not uncommon, especially with men. An erection is a normal reaction to certain stimuli."

"I know all about the parasympathetic nervous system and reaction to stimuli." His voice held a hint of anger that couldn't be ignored. "I also know my own body, and this has never happened to me before, at least not to this extent."

Erica worried that she'd subconsciously contributed to his discomfort. Had she been too light with her touch? Too curious? She'd learned how to deal with this very situation during her studies, but this was a man she secretly fantasized about—all the more reason why she shouldn't have agreed to the massage. "I could return to the therapeutic approach and apply more pressure, unless you'd prefer to stop now."

The smile he sent her was patently cynical. "No, I don't

want you to stop, but I think you better because no amount of pressure's going to cure me right now. At least not the kind you're offering."

"I'm sorry, Kieran," she said. "I didn't intend for this to happen."

He reached back and clasped her hand. "It's not your fault. Okay, indirectly it is your fault. But I'm not going to hold it against you."

"That's nice to know," she said after he released his hold on her. "What now?"

"Go change and get started on the treadmill. I'll be there as soon as I'm decent."

Chapter Seven

Right now Kieran could carry a three-hundred-pound weight across the parking lot, twice, and still struggle to remain decent. Short of attempting that feat, he'd done just about all he could do to calm himself down while coaching Erica, from bench-pressing to boxing the bag suspended in the corner of the room. He'd gone back to the weights again in an effort to work off more steam. Regardless, he was still on edge, barely hanging on to control. Nothing new there. He'd been avoiding that slippery slope since he'd met Erica. And the damn massage had nearly pushed him over the cliff.

Not that she'd done anything to encourage his reaction. But having her hands on his body, any part of his body, had been enough to contribute to his current state. He'd been a fool to think otherwise considering the nights he'd lain awake, fantasizing about her touching him, and not necessarily his back.

Since the workout had begun, Erica had been quiet, even

when he'd pressed her for more effort. She hadn't even argued with him once. He could only assume she suffered from as much discomfort as he did, and he felt damn guilty about that.

"I'm done," she called from the spin bike where she'd been going at it for a good twenty minutes. "What do you want me to do now?"

He could think of a few responses to that, none of which were respectable. After placing the barbell back on the rack, he sat up on the bench and swiped the back of his arm over his forehead. "That's all for tonight."

She slid off the bike and walked to the bench. "Are you sure? I still have forty-five minutes until I have to pick Stormy up from the party."

"Feel free to hang out here. I'm not going anywhere." Except insane, he realized when Erica took a drink of water and slid the tip of her tongue over her lips.

"I have an idea," she said. "I'm dying to see your apartment. You can give me the tour you promised."

"Sure." He'd answered too quickly. Apparently the process that had rerouted his blood supply from his brain to behind his fly prevented him from thinking clearly. But he couldn't very well rescind the offer now without having to explain why being alone with her wasn't such a hot idea.

When he failed to move, Erica stared down at him. "Since you've exercised enough to last a year, do I need to help you up?"

"No." He came to his feet to prove he didn't need her assistance. "And I've worked harder before." He was working hard now not to touch her.

"I'm sure you have." She took a fast glance around the room. "Where exactly is your apartment?"

"Right this way." He grabbed a towel en route to the door at the rear of the area. A towel might come in handy later, something he could stuff in his mouth when the temptation to kiss her stole his common sense.

After pounding out the code and releasing the lock, Kieran opened the door and gestured toward the staircase. "Up there, two flights."

Erica faced him and smiled. "What? No elevator?"

"Elevators are for people who either can't walk the stairs, or for those who won't walk. I don't qualify in either instance."

She held up her hands. "Okay, okay. You don't have to be so cranky."

He hadn't meant to be cranky, but his bad mood centered on his anger at himself, not at her. "I'll try to be nicer." But not too nice.

She followed him up the stairs and remained silent until he keyed in the code that unlocked the apartment. "I feel like we're about to enter the headquarters of the secret fitness police," she said. "No wonder you admire my alarm system."

Unable to hold back a smile, he opened the door and gestured her inside. "It's just your average, two-bedroom, two-bath apartment."

Erica strolled through the foyer and once in the great room, she turned a full circle before facing him again. "Average apartment? This is incredible. I love the contemporary look and I really love the spiral staircase."

Kieran tossed the towel on the back of the leather sofa. "It's okay, but not very practical when it comes to moving furniture." Maybe he should try moving some furniture up the stairs. Maybe then he could get his libido reined in. He opted instead to visit the built-in wet bar, intent on having a drink in an attempt to relax, and to put some distance between them. "Want a glass of wine?"

"That's not on my diet," she said. "But if it was, I'd love to have one."

He pulled a bottle of Bordeaux from the cabinet beneath the counter. "It's a red, and red wine's good for you, as long as you use some moderation."

"In that case, I'll have one glass, but don't fill it up since I'm driving."

While Kieran uncorked the bottle and poured the wine, Erica moved to the floor-to-ceiling windows that spanned the length of the room. "What a great view. Do you have the same view in your bedroom?" She looked back and smiled sheepishly. "Not that I'm suggesting I should check out your bedroom."

Luckily, he managed to carry the wine without dumping it all over the floor as he crossed the room and set the glasses on the coffee table. He started to say he had no problem with her checking out his bedroom, but quickly reconsidered. If he couldn't control his tongue—literally and figuratively— they could end up in an extremely compromising position. Asking her to join him on the sofa seemed the better part of valor, but before he could make the offer, she slid away the band binding her ponytail, causing her hair to cascade down her back. It dawned on him that he'd never seen her hair down before, and the sight was shredding what was left of his self-control.

He watched the sway of the deep copper-colored locks as she shook her head, like she held a pocket watch, bent on hypnotizing him. Frankly, it was working. And when she gathered her hair to pull it back up, he was at her back in a flash. "Leave it down," he said, causing her to drop her arm to her side.

He ran his hand over her hair and followed the waist-length strands down to their ends. Silk came to mind. Silk draped over his body when he made love to her. And damn it, he wanted that more than anything at the moment, even if he couldn't have it. But he had to have something, anything, which was the reason why he pulled her hair to one side and kissed her neck.

She shivered slightly before saying, "Kieran, your ethics—"

"I know." He took her by the shoulders and turned her around. "Right now, I don't give a damn about ethics." A sorry excuse for a man who prided himself on strength of will, even in the toughest situations. His will disappeared the moment he lowered his head and covered her mouth with his.

He backed Erica up against the window, not leaving even an inch of space between their bodies. She wrapped her arms around his neck while he rested his hands on her hips. And that's when the kiss became almost desperate—a mouth-to-mouth explosion that left nothing unexplored. When he'd kissed her before, and even when she'd kissed him, she hadn't gone full throttle. But now she gave as good as she got, and what she gave him could easily encourage him to start dispensing with the clothes. If she hadn't known the extent of his erection during the massage, then she sure as hell knew it now.

Kieran broke the kiss long enough to tell her, "I'm about to come unwound."

Erica blinked twice, as if trying to clear the mental fog. "This is insane, Kieran."

"Certifiably," he said as he attacked her neck again. "Crazy." Chemistry, the strongest he'd ever encountered.

Bracketing his jaws in her palms, she forced him to look at her. "We can't."

"I keep telling myself that, but I'm not listening." Unwilling to break all contact with her, he took a step back without dropping his hands from her waist. "But if you don't want this, you have to tell me now."

A sigh drifted from her lips. "Yes, I want this, right or wrong. But I have to pick up my daughter, remember?"

Hell, he'd be lucky to remember his name right now. "What time is it?"

"According to your clock, I have less than twenty minutes to get there."

"Twenty minutes wouldn't be nearly enough time to do what I want to do with you." When he noticed a glimpse of wariness in her eyes, he wondered if he'd gone too far this time. "What's wrong?"

"I'm just wondering why I always have my butt to the window for the entire world to see when I'm with you."

Leave it to her sense of humor to lighten the mood, only one of her many appealing qualities. "The windows are tinted, so you don't have to worry."

"At least that's one thing I don't have to worry about." She closed her eyes briefly and took a deep breath. "I am concerned over the way I behave around you. As much as I want this, I'm not sure how well I'll be able to handle the sex part."

For Kieran, it wasn't only about sex. If that were the case, then he could easily call any one of a select few female friends who'd be glad to put him out of his misery with a wild night and no commitment attached. Amazingly, he found that prospect unappealing, thanks to Erica—the only woman he wanted to spend the night with.

He pushed her hair behind one ear and pressed a kiss against her cheek. "Maybe we're making it more complicated than it has to be."

She lowered her hands to his chest but remarkably didn't push him away, at least not physically. "It is complicated. I have to consider Stormy and how she would feel about me being involved with a man. I need to seriously think about that."

Suddenly the earlier conversation with Candice came back to Kieran, illustrating how complicated it could get. Reinforcing why he shouldn't consider any personal involvement with

Erica, aside from the ethics issues. "You're probably right. There's one major problem neither of us counted on."

Now she looked almost alarmed. "What problem?"

He could barely think, much less communicate coherently, unless he put some space between them. Reluctantly releasing her, he strode to the sofa, collapsed onto the cushions and rubbed his temples. Apparently the blood flow had been redirected to his primary brain because he was getting one hell of a headache. After Erica claimed the chair across from him, he continued. "Candice stopped me when I dropped Stormy off. She asked me a few disturbing questions."

"Define *disturbing*."

"Disturbing in as she wanted to know if we were sleeping together."

Erica grabbed up a glass and took a long drink before setting it back on the table. "You did set her straight."

"Yeah, I did. But I don't know if that will discourage her from making assumptions." Assumptions that came close to being true a few moments before. "She could cause some problems."

"Including damaging your reputation."

He downed half of his wine in two gulps. "She could, but without proof, she doesn't have a leg to stand on. I'm more worried about you and Stormy. She might spread some rumors that could be tough to deal with."

When she didn't respond, he sat forward and draped his arms on his knees. "Look, Erica, the last thing I want to do is hurt you or Stormy. I could resign as your trainer and walk away, but I don't want to do that unless I have to."

She looked slightly panicked. "I don't want you to do that, either. I'm finally beginning to feel like my old self again, but I still need your help."

"Then let's finish what we started." After realizing how that might sound, he added, "In regard to your fitness program."

She rimmed the edge of the glass with a fingertip. "I realize that's what you meant. And the answer to our obvious inability to control ourselves would be to make sure we're not alone together."

He didn't necessarily like that proposition, but he'd have to live with it. "Good plan. No more alone time."

"No more massages, either," she said.

He couldn't deny his disappointment over that prospect. "Fine, and we'll make sure the kid is always around when we're together."

"Speaking of the kid." She finished off her wine and stood. "I'm anxious to see how the party went."

He saw the anxiety reflecting from her eyes. "You're still worried about the boy factor, aren't you?"

"Yes. Hopefully she showed more restraint than I did tonight."

On the drive home, Stormy's unwillingness to talk in anything but clipped sentences greatly concerned Erica. Her daughter's continued silence while she readied for bed only increased those concerns. "What happened at the party, sweetie?"

"Nothing happened, Mom."

She tucked the covers under Stormy's chin and perched on the edge of the bed. "You're awfully quiet. Are you sure nothing's wrong?"

Stormy wrested from the sheet and sat up against the headboard. "I don't like the way boys act sometimes."

Erica swallowed back the dread. "What did R.J. do to you?"

Stormy gave her the usual you-need-to-chill stare. "We didn't hook up or anything, if that's what you're worried about, Mom."

Hook up? "Do you even know what that means, Stormy?"

"Well, yeah. It means have sex."

As if Erica needed another reason not to sleep well tonight. "How much do you know about sex?"

Stormy lifted her chin. "I know what happens because Lisa's mom gave her a book and we read it together."

Erica had planned to purchase a similar book to give Stormy in the near future. Clearly she should have already done that. "Then you probably know that sex can be wonderful in a committed relationship, and that it can also be dangerous if you're not prepared, both emotionally and physically, for the responsibility."

Stormy blew out a breath of frustration. "I'm not going to have sex for a long time, so stop worrying, okay?"

At least that was something positive. Very positive, and a large load off Erica's mind, at least for the time being. "I'm glad to hear that, sweetie. But you still haven't told me what happened with you and R.J."

Stormy slapped a palm against her forehead, a sure sign she believed her mother was being obtuse. "When I said nothing happened, Mom, I meant *nothing* happened. Those dumb boys just stood around and stared at us all night."

Hard to kiss or "hook up" under those circumstances, thank heavens. "R.J. didn't talk to you at all?"

"He pretended he didn't even know me. Dumb, stupid boys."

Erica secretly celebrated the dumb boys on one hand, but hated that her daughter had been so disappointed on the other. "I promise there will come a time when they won't admire you from across the room." Someday soon, they would saunter across the room to garner her daughter's attention. She wasn't fond of that prospect, even though it was inevitable.

"And to make the night even worse, Lisa cried."

"The boys made her cry?"

Stormy folded the edge of the sheet back and forth. "She cried because her dad doesn't live with them anymore. I told her at least she still had a dad. I don't think that was the right thing to say to her because she cried even more."

Erica's heart went out to both her daughter and Lisa. "You did the best you could, sweetie. Just remember, it's going to take some time for her to adjust."

"She also said if her mom starts dating men, she'll run away from home. I told her that wasn't smart."

A good opportunity to pose the question that had plagued Erica since she'd left the health club. "What would you do if I decided to date again?"

Stormy looked totally shocked by the question. "Are you gonna date someone?"

"There isn't anyone right now." A bit of a white lie. If she did consider it, only one man came to mind, and he wasn't necessarily the right man. "But if I ever did decide to see someone, I'd like to know how you feel about it."

"If it was someone like Kieran, that would be okay."

If her daughter only knew how much she'd foolishly begun to want that. "Kieran's my personal trainer, Stormy, and that's all. As soon as I'm finished with my fitness training in a couple of weeks, he'll move on to someone else who needs his help." And as soon as she and Stormy accepted that, the better off they'd both be.

"He promised to help me with softball until tryouts," Stormy said. "He even told me he'd ask his sister to teach me how to pitch."

Erica didn't doubt Kieran would honor his promises, and that worried her because like it or not, her daughter had begun to view Kieran as a father figure, something she would have to discuss in detail with Stormy another time. The semi-sex talk had already drained her of the last of her energy.

"Time for bed, sweetie pie." She leaned over, kissed Stormy's forehead and stood, pausing a moment to relish the sight of her child, fresh faced and innocent, before that childhood was completely gone. "Sleep tight."

Before Erica could turn off the light, Stormy stopped her cold by saying, "I'm scared, Mom."

That sent Erica back to her child. "Scared of what, Stormy?"

Stormy looked as though she might cry. "I'm scared someday I won't remember what Daddy looks like."

Reclaiming her place on the bed, Erica blinked back her own tears. "That's why we have all the pictures, honey. So you don't forget."

"Do you still remember, Mom? I mean, do you remember how he sounded? I used to, but I don't now."

"Yes, I still remember." She remembered the sound of Jeff's laughter, although he hadn't laughed all that much during the years after Stormy's birth. Neither had she. She remembered the harshness of his tone when he'd been frustrated and the gentleness of his voice when he'd spoken to his baby girl. She recalled how hard the times had been. How they'd become virtual strangers before his death, and how much she'd hated the emotional berth that had developed between her and the man she'd always considered her best friend.

Yet tonight, when she'd been in Kieran's arms, she'd forgotten it all, and that's when the guilt hit her like an unexpected slap in the face.

Erica automatically touched the silver chain she wore around her neck, the one that held her wedding band, and vowed to remember, no matter what the future held. Vowed to remember all the good times, not the bad, because there had been many good times before Stormy's illness had stripped them of their youthfulness. Before fate had cruelly ripped Jeff from their lives before he could enjoy his child's return to health. Before they could set their marriage back on solid ground, as it had been in the beginning.

Simply stated, life wasn't always fair. And the most unfair part of all—like Stormy's own father, eventually Kieran O'Brien would be out of their lives for good. But until that time came, she would enjoy the moments they spent together and deal with the possible fallout later.

Over the next week, Kieran and Stormy settled into a routine, traveling to the batting cages in the afternoons while Erica was still at work, playing catch in the evenings before they all went to the club for Erica's workout. Kieran had also fallen behind on some of his responsibilities, but it had all been worth it, if only to witness Stormy's pride over her accomplishments. If only to see Erica, even if he couldn't touch her. He still wanted to touch her, even after he followed Stormy into the house one day and found Erica sitting on the sofa, the cordless phone clutched in her hand, a troubled look on her face.

For a minute he worried that he'd done something wrong to contribute to her distress when she didn't bother to look up after Stormy proclaimed, "I hit six balls in a row, Mom!"

"That's great, sweetie."

Stormy frowned. "Are you okay, Mom?"

Erica sent her a weak smile. "I'm fine. Just a little tired."

"Can I call Lisa and tell her what I did?" she asked, apparently satisfied that her mother was okay, although Kieran knew better.

Erica leaned over and set the phone back on the charger on the end table. "Dinner's almost ready, and you need to finish your homework before you make any phone calls."

"I hate homework. Homework should be outlawed." After strongly stating her opinions, Stormy strode out of the room, leaving Kieran and Erica alone for the first time since the week before in his apartment.

Erica looked up at him and sighed. "I've had a really bad day. Do you mind if I skip the gym tonight? I'll make it up tomorrow."

Kieran took a seat beside her, raked the baseball cap off his head and draped one arm over the back of the couch. "What's wrong?"

She seemed almost startled by the question. "Nothing's wrong."

"Don't hand me that, Erica. I noticed the minute I walked into the room."

She tipped her head back on the sofa and stared at the ceiling. "I had a phone call from Jeff's mother right before you got here. She wants us to spend Thanksgiving weekend with her in Tulsa. Since Jeff's dad passed away three years ago, she refuses to drive long distances, so she hasn't seen Stormy in almost two years."

"Sounds like a nice way to spend the holiday." He put as much enthusiasm as he could muster into his tone, even though he was less than enthused about her four-day absence. Her fitness goals would suffer. He would suffer from not being with her, although he wasn't going to own up to that.

She shifted to face him. "I can't go. I have appointments scheduled for Friday after the holiday and half the day Saturday. I can't afford to cancel them."

Kieran couldn't quell his relief. "I'm sure she'll understand."

"She still wants Stormy to come even if I can't. If I give the go-ahead, she's willing to buy her a plane ticket, and she has limited income. That's how badly she wants to see her. But then, Stormy's the only grandchild."

As much as he wanted to discourage her from taking the trip, he couldn't do it. "Are you sure you can't reschedule your appointments?"

She picked at a random thread jutting from the sofa's arm. "It's not only the money. It's difficult for me to be around Nancy. I practically grew up in that house, and she's turned it into a shrine, understandably so, since Jeff was their only child. But it's not easy, dealing with all the memories, and that's incredibly selfish on my part."

Kieran wasn't immune to selfishness, since he wanted her to stay in town. He wasn't impervious to jealousy, either, something he realized when he experienced envy of the former man in her life. A man who was no longer alive but still had a strong hold on her. He wondered if her husband had appreciated Erica's remarkable qualities, her devotion. If he had made her happy.

Shaking off the thoughts, he asked, "Are you going to let her go?"

Finally, she met his gaze. "I probably should. She'll also have the opportunity to see my parents since they practically live next door to Nancy. But Stormy's never flown alone before. And the thought of putting her on a plane all by herself with a bunch of strangers scares me. I realize kids do it all the time. Just not my kid."

She did have a point, Kieran decided. And he had an idea that could be the answer to her fears, at least in part. "Would you let her go if she went by private plane?"

Erica laughed. "Unfortunately, mine's hired out next Thursday."

"I'm serious. My brother Logan owns a global-transportation company and he's recently added a new fleet of jets. It'll take one phone call and he'll have a plane ready to fly her to Tulsa. She'll have her own personal crew and you won't have to worry about her getting lost in a crowd."

Her mouth dropped open before she snapped it closed again. "You're serious?"

"Yeah, I am." Of course, he hadn't asked his brother yet, but that shouldn't be a problem. Logan had the money and the means to accommodate the request. "I'll even take you to the airport on Thursday morning to see her off."

She sat silent, mulling it over for a moment before she asked, "She'll have her own crew?"

"You bet, including at least one flight attendant. I could request a bartender and chef, but since she's underage, and the flight won't be that long, that's probably overkill."

She smiled. "You're right about that. And if you can do this, it would save Nancy from having to pay for a last-minute ticket." Her smile faded into a frown. "Is this going to cost you?"

Not monetarily speaking, but Logan could come up with a creative payback, like making him clean out the plane prior to its departure just to have a good laugh. "Logan owes me for the time I took the blame for a baseball he tossed through our mother's kitchen window."

"Speaking of baseballs," she said. "Aside from hitting six balls in a row, how's Stormy doing with everything else?"

"Damn good. She has a strong arm and great hand-eye coordination. One of these days, I'm going to take her to my sister to see if she has the mechanics and makeup to be a pitcher."

"Stormy mentioned that to me last week." Erica laid a hand on his arm. "You've done so much already, so please don't feel obligated to do more."

He wasn't doing anything out of obligation. He was doing it because he cared for both of them, much more than he should. "Mallory will get a kick out of revisiting her old softball days. Plus she needs to get in some practice for when her girls are old enough to play." Which was still a good three years away, but knowing Mallory and Whit, they'd have the twins running bases by midsummer.

When Erica fell silent, Kieran decided she was still stuck on the whole private-plane offer. "Do you want me to make the call to Logan, or do you want more time to think about it?"

Indecision passed over her face, replaced by acquiescence. "You can make the call, as long as you're sure it's not going to be an imposition on your brother."

"Deal."

"Okay, then." Erica slapped her hands on her thighs and rose from the couch. "I have chicken in the oven that should be done about now. Can you stay for dinner?"

He could, but he needed to get back to the club and do some analysis—of his business's finances and his feelings for Erica.

Kieran stood and replanted the cap on his head. "I've got some paperwork that needs my attention. But thanks for the offer."

"I appreciate you and everything you've done for us. More than you realize."

When Erica slid her arms around his waist and laid her head on his chest, Kieran automatically wrapped his own arms around her. For a long moment, they stood there, holding each other, until Erica backed away, much to Kieran's disappointment.

"I'll see you tomorrow night," she said.

"Tomorrow night it is." But before he left, he had one more thing to say. "Allowing Stormy to go on this trip alone is a positive step, Erica."

"I know. Pretty amazing for a woman who has trouble letting her child stay by herself for more than an hour."

Everything about her amazed him—from her deep dimples to her devious sense of humor. Unable to help himself, Kieran leaned over to kiss her cheek. "Just remember, when you see Stormy off next week, I'll be right there with you."

Chapter Eight

Once they arrived at the municipal airport Thanksgiving morning, Kieran's support was the only thing holding Erica together. She would need that continued support in the next few minutes when she would send her daughter on a journey, alone. And if she could do that without bawling, well, that would be simply short of a miracle. Stormy, on the other hand, seemed more than ready to board the plane without her mother. An incredible plane, Erica concluded, from the looks of the dark blue streamlined jet sitting on the tarmac outside the waiting-area windows. She didn't care how it looked, as long as it functioned properly.

Instead of dwelling on the negatives, she chose to think positive thoughts while Kieran conversed with Logan, whose dark good looks served as another reminder of the prime O'Brien genes. A few moments later, a fortysomething debonair man and a pretty, tall blonde approached the group, introducing themselves as the pilot and attendant in charge of Stormy's flight.

"My name is Muriel," the woman said as she offered her hand to Erica for a shake. "I'll take good care of your daughter."

She was counting on that. "This is only her second plane ride and the only one she's taken alone. I doubt she even remembers the first flight." The flight they'd taken to Oklahoma for Jeff's funeral, a sorrowful trip Erica would never forget.

"I do too remember, Mom." She looked up at the lady and smiled. "They gave me a wing pin. I still have it in my jewelry box at home."

"We don't have any of those, Stormy," Muriel said. "But we do have a whole refrigerator full of chocolate milk."

Stormy rocked back and forth on her heels, barely containing her excitement. "That's my favorite drink. Can we go now?"

"They're ready if you are," Kieran said, his comment aimed at Erica.

Was she ready? Not really. But they'd come this far, she couldn't change her mind now. "Sure." She turned back to the attendant. "Stormy has her grandmother's phone number in her backpack, although I'm certain she'll be waiting when you arrive."

"I'll personally give her a call right after we touch down," Muriel said. "I'll call you, too. I have a son who's a little older than Stormy, so I know how important it is for you to know she's safe."

Thank goodness for the kindness of strangers who also happened to be mothers. "I appreciate that."

Kieran tugged on one of Stormy's curls. "Tell your mom goodbye, kiddo."

Without hesitating, Stormy threw her arms around Erica's waist and grinned. "Thanks for letting me go, Mom. We'll

have a party together when I get back to celebrate—uh—
Thanksgiving."

Erica knew exactly what Stormy had almost said before
she'd reconsidered. A very wise decision since she'd been
forewarned not to mention her mother's birthday to anyone.
"You have a nice visit with Nana Stevens. Give her a kiss and
hug for me, and tell your Granddad and Grandma Keller we'll
see them at Christmas."

"I will."

With a heavy heart and tears threatening to spill from her
eyes, Erica watched Muriel take Stormy's hand in hers and
walk away. She continued to watch until her baby disappeared through the door that didn't allow Erica admittance,
reminding her of all the surgeries where she'd entrusted
Stormy to the care of professionals because she'd had no
choice. Stormy had survived then, and she'd do so now. That
still didn't soothe the ache or tamp down her urge to chase
after her child before she boarded the plane.

"She'll be fine," Kieran said, giving her some much-
needed reassurance.

"I know she will, but it's still hard."

"Mark Henry's clocked thousands of hours of flight time,"
Logan added. "He's the best pilot I have."

Erica swallowed around the yet-to-dissipate lump in her
throat. "I really do appreciate this, Logan. I hope it wasn't too
much trouble."

Logan smiled a smile much like Kieran's. "No trouble at
all. And if you're ever interested in leaving the spa, I have
several corporate clients who request onboard massage thera-
pists, particularly on international flights. If you're as good
as Kieran says you are, I'd hire you in a heartbeat."

"She's not interested, Logan."

Kieran's abrupt and somewhat irritable dismissal took

Erica aback. "I can speak for myself, Kieran," she said. "But he is right, Logan. As much as I appreciate the offer, I couldn't be away from Stormy that long."

"Let me know if you change your mind." Logan pushed up his sleeve and took a quick check of his watch. "I've got to pick up Jenna and J.D. before I head over to Mom and Dad's. You're going to be there, right?"

"You bet," Kieran said. "I wouldn't want to miss Mom's pumpkin pie."

"How about you, Erica?" Logan asked. "Do you have any plans?"

"Well, no, but I—"

"She's coming with me, Logan."

Erica stared at Kieran. "Since when?"

"Since I decided you don't need to be at home alone, worrying about the kid. My mother cooks enough to feed the entire community of West Houston, so there'll be plenty of food."

Great. Nothing like being tempted to blow the diet. But she honestly liked the thought of spending time with Kieran's family. "As long as she serves celery, that might be an option."

"Like I've told you before, moderation is the key," Kieran said. "And if you slip up, I'll make you work extra hard tomorrow evening."

"I'll see you both in about an hour, then." Logan started down the corridor before turning and walking backward. "It was nice meeting you, Erica. And don't let this guy talk you into a nooner. My mother expects everyone there on time."

Erica was rendered speechless while Kieran added, "Don't listen to him. He's full of it, just like the rest of my brothers."

"I'm so glad to know you're not going to try to engage me in a *nooner,*" she said as soon as Logan was out of earshot, though the thought wasn't at all repulsive.

"Actually, I was going to say my mother wouldn't care if we were a few minutes late."

She planted a playful slap on his arm. "I haven't even agreed to go with you yet."

He responded with a sly, crooked grin. "Anything I can do to convince you?"

Spending the day with Kieran was all the convincing Erica needed. "I'll go, as long as you promise you won't make me run behind the car after lunch."

"Promise." He draped an arm around her shoulder. "But just a word of warning. Spending time with the O'Briens is like spending a day at the zoo."

The minute they'd stepped through the door two hours ago, Kieran realized he'd thrown Erica into a den of fawning lions. Lions who meant well, but still a little too feral with their enthusiasm. At least she hadn't run out the door…yet.

Although he'd brought women home before—two to be exact—neither had earned as much attention. But then neither had been as personable as Erica. She'd played on the floor with the babies, helped prepare lunch and overall, blended in with the siblings as if she'd been taking part in their gatherings all her life. More important, Erica was a huge hit with his mother and father, who likely viewed her as the perfect daughter-in-law prospect. Lucy probably expected to see her every Sunday from this point forward, and Dermot would expect his son to propose to her by the end of the day.

An occasional Sunday dinner might work, but having her as a permanent part of their lives—his life—was a stretch. Yet during the meal, as he'd watched her from across the dinner table, her hair falling past her shoulders and her dimples on exhibit, he could easily envision her there every week. He could picture Stormy playing big sister to the nieces and nephews, tossing a softball around in the backyard with Mallory. He could imagine taking Erica home afterward, making love to her late into the night and… Damn, he was in trouble.

Kieran chalked up his suddenly sappy disposition to his mother's announcement that Erica had made the sweet potato casserole from her own recipe. He was a sucker for good cooking, the only way he could explain his visions of domestic bliss. He didn't care to examine the other possible reasons. Not until he got the hell away from family central.

Now that the meal had been devoured, the kitchen cleaned through a concerted effort and the babies put down for a nap, only a few returned to the table for dessert. Devin had left for his in-laws with Stacy and the boys over an hour ago, while Aidan, Logan and Whit, along with their wives, were out in the yard partaking in the traditional touch football game. And of course, his mother was still in the kitchen, doing who knew what.

That left Erica, his dad and of all people, Kevin, who was conveniently seated across from Kieran, right next to Erica. The fact his twin had bothered to make an appearance, and hadn't tried to hit on Erica, meant the devil must be doling out ice cubes.

Kieran couldn't help but wonder over Kevin's uncharacteristic silence, the fact that he looked like he hadn't slept in weeks. He'd apparently lost his razor, too. Strange, since his twin normally prided himself on immaculate grooming.

Kieran could only surmise that his brother had had one crazy, sex-filled night with his current woman, if she was still in the picture. No way of knowing that unless he asked, and he didn't plan to ask.

When Kevin kept staring at his untouched dessert plate, Kieran couldn't leave well enough alone, thanks to the latent anger he retained over his brother's poor choices. "Hard living's starting to take its toll on you, Kev. You look like hell."

Kieran waited for the usual acerbic comeback, but Kevin only muttered, "You're right about that."

Damn. He was much worse off than Kieran had realized if he couldn't do better than that. "I know you think sleep's overrated, but you ought to try it sometime."

His mother returned to the table and served up a scowl, along with a piece of pie to his father. "It's Thanksgiving, so both of you please call a truce. Little Maddie and Lucy get along better than the two of you when you're together, and they're toddlers."

"Sorry," Kieran muttered, and he honestly was. He had no business ruining his mother's holiday because he couldn't forgive and forget his brother's transgressions.

In typical subject-changing fashion, his dad said, "Tell us about your girl, Erica. Would she be havin' your red hair?"

Erica smiled. "She's more blond than red."

"Well, I'd be assumin' you're Irish."

"Actually, my maiden name is Keller. I've been told I get my coloring from my German great-grandmother, but I do have distant cousins named McCann."

Dermot slapped a palm on the table, rattling the remaining silverware. "I knew it."

Time to intervene. "As far as my dad's concerned, everyone should be Irish," Kieran said. "And those who aren't should wish they were."

Dermot looked exceedingly insulted. "I have nothin' against the Germans, Kieran. I'm only sayin' that our Erica here has Irish blood flowin' through her veins, I am sure of it."

Our Erica. For Kieran, that about said it all.

The back door slammed and in walked Mallory, her auburn hair pulled up in a ponytail, looking a lot like the little sister Kieran remembered from years back. "What's up?" she asked as she took the other unoccupied chair next to Erica.

"We're discussing Erica's daughter," Kieran offered, along with a look that said to jump right in before their father got on a roll.

"We were discussin' Erica's hair color," Dermot said. "Would it be natural, lamb?"

Kevin failed to comment, Kieran silently cursed and Mallory rolled her eyes. "I can't believe you asked that, Dad," she said. "You better be glad Mom didn't hear you."

"I heard him," came Lucy's voice from the kitchen. "Behave yourself, old man, or I'll send all the leftovers home with the children."

Dermot tossed his napkin aside and grumbled. "The woman has ears like a wolfhound."

Erica didn't look at all shocked. In fact, she laughed. "In answer to your question, I've had the same hair color since the day I was born."

After sending their dad a quelling look she'd learned from their mother, Mallory shifted toward Erica. "Kieran tells me Stormy's a good athlete."

Erica's smile showed her pride. "That's what I understand, although she's just now started working on her softball skills."

"I'd be glad to help her if you'd like," Mallory said.

Lucy reclaimed the chair next to her husband. "Mallory was quite the pitcher in high school."

"That she was," Dermot said. "You'd do well to take her up on the offer."

Erica took a sip of diet soda. "Stormy would love that. We'll be glad to work around your schedule, Mallory."

"Sounds great," Mallory said. "I'll call you next week."

Just like that, Erica had agreed without any argument. Kieran realized how far she'd come in the few weeks he'd known her, that she'd finally begun to view her daughter as a healthy, normal kid.

Dermot cocked his head to one side and asked Lucy, "What do you have cookin' in the oven, darlin'? You've already prepared more than enough to choke a jackass."

Lucy's expression turned somber. "It's not for us, my love. I've baked a cake to take to the Garzas this evening. The children will be coming in tonight to plan the funeral."

Kieran didn't have a clue what his mother was talking about. "Whose funeral, and who are the Garzas?"

"Ignacio Garza's funeral. He passed away yesterday in his sleep. I volunteer with his wife, Nita, down at the library."

"From what I know, Ignacio was a good man," Dermot added. "He could grow a fine garden, he could. Your mother used to bring home a bushel of his tomatoes every summer. I'll dearly be missin' his tomatoes."

"His wife will miss him," Lucy said. "They were married over fifty years."

Kevin abruptly pushed back from the table and headed for the kitchen, plate in hand, before disappearing altogether.

Kieran wasn't surprised. His brother had never cared to converse about death.

Lucy leaned forward, lowered her voice and said, "Don't you think Kevin looks terribly pale? He's also acting strangely."

Kieran didn't disagree with his mother, but he didn't want to discuss it, either. "He looks tired, Mom, and that's all. He probably had an out-of-town trip last week." And pulled an all-nighter on top of that.

Dermot patted Lucy's arm. "Leave the boy be, Lucine. You don't have to mollycoddle him now that he's a grown man."

Lucy flipped a hand in dismissal, as if to say she was going to do what she wanted anyway. To Kieran, that meant worrying about his twin to her usual extreme. "Anyway, as I was saying," she continued. "Nita and Ignacio have been everything to each other. I worry over how she's going to take losing him, especially at this time of the year."

"It's horrible to lose a spouse any time," Mallory said. "Much less the day before a holiday."

Kieran recognized they'd entered territory Erica had personally charted. A place she obviously didn't want to visit, judging from her lowered eyes and lack of participation in the dialogue. But before he could spin the conversation in a different direction to prevent her from enduring more talk of loss, his mother added, "The worst of it is, I don't know what to say to Nita."

"I know what you mean," Mallory said. "When one of the senior partners at the law office lost his wife two years ago, I didn't have a clue how I should act or what I should say."

"It's okay if you don't say anything at all."

At the sound of Erica's voice, all attention turned to her, and Kieran damned himself for not stopping the conversation sooner.

"The most important thing is just being there to listen," she continued. "Providing that proverbial shoulder to cry on. But sometimes you only want to be alone with your grief and you think you're being selfish. Maybe everyone else believes that, too. Still, you have to have that alone time to survive."

No one tried to interrupt as Erica went on, seemingly lost in a reality that Kieran had never experienced. "Those phases of grief, the anger, sadness, it's all true. But eventually acceptance does happen when one day you look at your child and you realize the memories will always live on in the loved ones who've been left behind."

She paused for a moment, a noticeable dampness in her eyes, before she straightened her shoulders and sighed.

"Anyway, before I went off on that, I meant to say that you don't have to worry about saying the wrong thing. 'I'm sorry' and 'I'm here for you' both work well."

For a long stretch of time, no one said a word, including Kieran. Until that moment, he hadn't understood the magnitude of her pain. He only wanted to hold her, but before he could move, his mother slid into the chair Kevin had vacated and hugged Erica. "Thank you, dear. That was very sound advice. And I'm so sorry if we've upset you. We weren't being considerate of your situation."

Erica's smile was soft and sincere. "It's okay, Lucy. If we can't share our own experiences with friends, then who can we share them with?"

"You're a brave lass, Erica," Dermot said, looking a little misty himself.

"I agree," Mallory added.

Erica shook her head. "Believe me, I've had some cowardly moments. Just ask Kieran how I reacted the first time he told me I had to run five blocks."

They all shared in a laugh before Kieran said, "She handled it like a trooper. In fact, she's taken everything I've thrown at her with more guts than most of my clients."

They exchanged a look of understanding, until the sound of a crying baby interrupted the moment.

Mallory pushed back from the table and stood. "That's Maddie, and that's my cue to take the girls home. They're still not feeling all that well, thanks to their colds. Logan's going to bring Whit home later."

"I hate to see you go, dear," Lucy said. "But I do understand."

Mallory slapped a palm against her forehead. "I forgot to say the guys are waiting for you, Kieran. You're supposed to take my place."

"Mallory, would it be too much trouble for you to drop me

by my house on your way out?" Erica asked. "It's only a couple of miles away."

Mallory smiled. "Not a problem, as long as you have a high tolerance for two fussy toddlers."

Kieran came to his feet. "I'll take you home."

Erica waved him off. "I don't want to mess up your football game."

"They can wait."

She stood. "Really, you should stay and enjoy the rest of the day."

"It's no trouble for me to take her, Kieran," Mallory said. "Then you can go about the business of being macho and preening with the boys."

Kieran wanted to issue another protest, to argue the point, but when Mallory gave him a "back off" stare, that's exactly what he did—backed off. "Fine. I'll walk you out."

"That's not necessary." She gestured toward the back door. "Go play some football. Just don't put yourself out of commission before we finish my program."

"I insist on walking you out." His irritable tone earned him a hard look from his mother.

"Would you like for me to fix you a plate to take home, Erica?" Lucy asked. "You ate so little at lunch."

Erica shook her head. "As much as I'd love to, I can't. I'm trying to take pounds off, not put them on."

"Don't be thinkin' you need to lose weight, girlie." Dermot patted his belly and rose from the chair. "Now me, I could use to shed a few. But first, I think I'll be havin' me another piece of pie."

Dermot doled out a bear hug to Erica, which she accepted without hesitation, before he headed off to his favorite place—the kitchen.

Erica addressed Lucy without looking at Kieran. "Thank

you for having me. It's been wonderful, sharing the holiday with such a great family."

Lucy drew Erica into an embrace. "It's been our pleasure, and we expect you to be back soon. And next time, bring your daughter. We'd love to meet her."

Mallory sent a quick glance Kieran's direction. "Mom, could you help me with the girls while Kieran tells Erica goodbye? I'll meet you two at the car."

Erica left the room in a hurry, pausing only to snatch her purse from the end table while Kieran followed her onto the porch. Once there, she leaned against a column, like she needed it for support. "I had a good time, Kieran. I'm glad I came."

He braced a hand on the beam, right above her head. "Hope you're not making a quick exit because you're too over-whelmed."

"Not at all. I just need to get home to gear up for tomorrow."

"Are you sure you don't want me to take you home? We could kick back and watch a movie. Make some popcorn." Make out.

"And we'd be all alone, which is why you can't come home with me. That's the rule, remember?"

Damn the rules. And damn if she wasn't right. With Stormy gone, nothing would prevent them from taking advantage of the situation. They'd already proven they couldn't rely on their willpower. "You're right, but if you change your mind, call me. I'll try to behave myself."

She smiled. "I'm sure you would, and so would I. I'm also certain the price of gas will drop below a dollar a gallon tomorrow."

The screen door opened, preventing Kieran from pushing Erica into changing her mind. Probably a good thing, other-wise they might make a huge mistake, although he didn't view being with her as a mistake. And that was a notion he needed to take out and scrutinize later.

"We're all ready," Mallory announced. "Say goodbye to Uncle Kieran."

Kieran glanced at the door to see Mallory with Lucy braced on one hip and his mother carting Maddie in her arms. He walked over and planted a kiss on Lucy's cheek, then did the same to Maddie. "You girls don't give your mom too much trouble on the way home."

Maddie grabbed a handful of his hair and giggled, and so did the trio of women surrounding him. Once he dislodged his niece before she sculpted him a nice bald spot in his scalp, he gave his mother a quick hug. "I'll see you a week from Sunday."

She frowned. "We're still having lunch at Mallory's this Sunday."

"I'm going to take a rain check," he said. "I've got some work to catch up on." Although he needed a break from the togetherness, he wasn't lying about his neglected work.

"If you must." Lucy stepped off the porch with Mallory trailing behind her, but when Erica moved to follow, Kieran took her arm to halt her progress. He leaned over and whispered, "Remember, call me if you change your mind."

"I admire your persistence, but I'm not going to call you."

Kieran released his hold on her and watched as she swayed down the walkway to the car. He instantly went back in the house, knowing that if he stayed and took the good long look he'd wanted to take, he'd give himself away. Then he'd have to hear about it from his sister from now until the lights went out on the universe.

Kieran pushed out the back door to find Whit, Aidan and Logan sitting in the lawn chairs set out on the patio, not a female to be found. He grabbed the discarded football from the grass and tossed it up with one hand. "I realize Mallory cut out, but where are the rest of the O'Brien women?"

"Corri's feeding the baby," Aidan said.

"Jenna's lying down," Logan added. "She says she's queasy, but I'm not sure why. We ate the same things and I feel fine."

Kieran pointed at Aidan. "What did I tell you?"

Aidan grinned and high-fived Kieran. "Another O'Brien bun in the oven."

Logan looked extremely incensed. "You don't know what the hell you're talking about!"

"Yeah, right," Kieran said. "Anyone know where Kevin is?"

"He's also taking a nap. He must have one helluva hangover." Logan stood and held out his hands. "Give me the ball."

Kieran threw it to Logan, nearly knocking him backward, prompting Logan to utter a few choice words that would send their mother for the soap.

Aidan left his chair and sprinted out farther into the yard. "Where's Erica?"

When Logan threw the ball back to Kieran, he passed it to Aidan. "Mallory took her home. She has to get ready for work tomorrow."

Aidan stopped midpass to stare at Kieran. "And you didn't go with her?"

"Let me get this straight," Logan said. "You have a good-looking, smart, funny redhead at your disposal, the kid's out of the state, and you're here, playing catch with your brothers instead of taking part in some afternoon delight with your girl-friend? Something's definitely wrong with that picture."

He understood why Logan would consider him a fool for letting Erica leave without him. He'd questioned it himself. But the answer was easy—she'd refused his offer. He damn sure wasn't going to admit that and opted for the logical reason for not suggesting some "afternoon delight." "She's a client, not my girlfriend."

Aidan chuckled as he passed the ball back to Kieran. "If you look at all your clients the way you look at Erica, I'm surprised you ever get anything accomplished."

Putting all his strength behind the pass, Kieran shot the ball to Aidan, who dropped it immediately. "Go to hell, Aidan. You don't know anything about what's going on with Erica."

"Yeah, he does," Logan said. "And so do I. You want her in a bad way. Problem is, she doesn't want you."

Problem was, they wanted each other in a real bad way. "Not that it's any of your business, but we've both decided to keep it professional between us. Less complicated that way."

Aidan kicked the ball aside and rejoined the group. "It's like I told you before, Kieran. If you want it, go for it, and figure out the rest later. You've never turned your back on a challenge, so why start now?"

Erica was definitely a challenge, that much Kieran knew. All his determination to keep things strictly business between them had lost its logic and luster. He'd always preferred walking the straight and narrow, but he'd begun to venture off the path from the moment he'd kissed her. He was tired of overanalyzing their relationship. Tired of going to bed fantasizing about her when all he wanted was the reality. Tired of fighting his feelings for her.

That reality might be within his reach, as soon as he found a way to be alone with her again. First and foremost, he had to convince her to talk to him.

Chapter Nine

"Your birthday's tomorrow."

That was the strangest phone greeting Erica had ever received, coming from the sexiest voice she'd ever encountered. "Hello to you, too, Kieran. And if Stormy told you about my birthday, I'm going to have to tape her mouth shut when she gets back."

"She didn't say a thing. I found it in your file when I verified your phone number."

Of course. He practically had her entire life history in that file. "By the way, I wear a size five shoe, in case you want to fill in the only detail you don't know."

His laugh was low, persuasive. Sexy. "What do you want for your birthday?"

"I want everyone to forget about it."

"Sorry. Can't do that."

"Seriously, Kieran. You've given me more than enough,

with the training and the plane ride. Stormy's softball. The list goes on and on."

"I'm talking about dinner between friends in a restaurant with cloth napkins."

He was darned determined to lure her in like a humming-bird to sugar water. "What about my workout?"

"We can vary the routine. I'll pick you up from the spa tomorrow afternoon and after your workout, we'll have a light meal. Maybe seafood. Crab and lobster."

Erica's stomach began to rumble just thinking about having a platter of cold boiled shrimp. Luckily, she could eat shrimp and still adhere to her diet. "I suppose I could take you up on the offer."

"Good. Bring extra clothes for dinner."

"I guess I could shower at the club, right?"

"Or my place."

As tempting as that sounded, going anywhere near his apartment again wasn't such a hot proposition—correction—it was a *hot* proposition. "We'll figure it out tomorrow."

"Then it's a date. I'll see you tomorrow."

A date? That was an interesting concept.

She had one more thing to cover before he hung up. "I want to apologize for my behavior at your parents' today. I didn't mean to get all weepy on you."

"Don't worry about it. My parents fell in love with you the minute you walked into the kitchen and started cooking."

And she'd fallen in love with them, too. If she wasn't careful, she could fall in love with their son. The thought stunned her into silence.

"Erica, are you still there?"

"Yes. Sorry. I thought I might sneeze." Or sink to the floor from shock. "Your family's wonderful. I now understand where you come by your generosity."

"My mother's always stressed it's important to give when you have it to give. And by the way, my dad's still convinced you're an Irish princess."

Happy-go-lucky Dermot. Erica had never met anyone quite like him, and probably never would again. "The next time I'm home, I'll be sure to inquire over my lineage to see if I can claim any Irish royalty. If not, I'll make something up."

Again, Kieran laughed. And again, Erica reveled in the sound of his laughter. "I'll let you go," he said. "Unless you've decided you want some company tonight."

"It's almost midnight."

"Which means I could officially wish you a happy birthday if I leave now."

How very tempting to tell him yes, but she wasn't certain she was ready for the possibilities. "I wasn't born until 5:42 p.m., so you'd be premature in your wishes. I tend to stretch it out as long as possible."

"Then I'll give you my official pronouncement when I see you tomorrow."

"I'm looking forward to it." And she was, very much so.

"Any kind of celebration planned at the spa?" he asked.

"Heavens, I hope not."

"Happy birthday, Erica!"

She should have known something was up when she'd come downstairs to find the salon practically deserted. She should have known she wouldn't be allowed to slip by one year without facing the customary spa celebration. As predicted, most of her fellow employees were present in the break room, huddled around the table that contained a large fruit plate with a question-mark candle stuck in the center. If they really believed she was going to give up her age, they had another think coming.

Resigned to her fate, Erica hugged each of the stylists and delivered the usual "You shouldn't have."

Bette slid an arm around her waist. "We wouldn't forget, sugar."

She sincerely wished they had. "The fruit plate's great, and thanks for not getting me any gifts."

"Oh, but we did." Megan pulled out a silver and blue gift bag from beneath the table. "We all chipped in and got you this."

Erica was afraid to look. Last year she'd been bestowed with a pair of large Christmas-tree earrings that actually lit up. Bette's idea, of course. She'd only worn them once, for politeness' sake, because she didn't care to have her ear lobes illuminated like a billboard.

Moving the tissue paper aside, Erica reached into the bag and contacted silk. When she drew the item out, she hoped for a nice, tasteful scarf. What she got was an oversize handkerchief with straps. A zebra-striped print handkerchief, no less.

She held the negligee up, encouraging one stylist to squeal and the rest to applaud, much to Erica's chagrin. She didn't want to seem ungrateful. Honestly, she didn't, but she couldn't halt the comment. "This is going to look great on one of my thighs."

"Nonsense," Bette said. "Your clothes are hanging off you, sugar. Why, you could put a marching band in your britches."

Bette was well known for her exaggerations, but that one topped them all. True, Erica had lost a few inches, something she'd learned when she'd spent her lunch break shopping for a special outfit for tonight. She'd even bought a skirt a whole size smaller. But that didn't mean she could actually wear this naughty nighty, or stick a marching band in her pants. Besides, she didn't have any cause to wear sexy lingerie, and no one to wear it for, unless…

"If you haven't gotten laid yet, honey, this should do the trick."

Leave it to Bette to contribute to Erica's already intense mortification.

When a rap came at the door, Erica looked up to find the new appointment clerk standing immediately inside the break room. "What's up, Joanie?" Bette asked.

"There's this great-looking guy here asking for Erica. Did someone hire a stripper?"

Clearly Kieran had arrived. "He's not a stripper. He's my… Never mind."

"Send him back," Bette said. "I'll convince him to take off his clothes."

Erica shoved the negligee back into the bag. "You'll do no such thing. And tell him to wait for me in the reception area, Joanie. I'll be right with him."

Bette winked. "Big night with the pizza man?"

"I'm not going to answer that." And she didn't. Instead, she breezed out of the break room and sprinted up the stairs to the therapy room to retrieve her duffel along with the garment bag holding her new outfit. She shoved the dubious gift into the duffel, where it would remain until she arrived safely back home. That was the last thing she needed, giving Kieran the impression she was packing seduction wear.

After returning to the first floor, Erica discovered Kieran leaning against the front desk, wearing a basic navy tee and jeans, and chatting with Joanie, who looked as if she might drool all over the appointment book.

"Let's go," she said without formality, and without looking at him.

Right outside the door, she spotted Kieran's Porsche parked a few spaces away and headed that direction. Finally, she would get to ride in the ideal vehicle with the ideal man.

After they settled into the car and buckled up, Kieran

dangled one arm over the steering wheel and studied her for a long moment. "Are you okay?"

She put on an exaggerated grin. "I'm great. Just peachy. A year older, too."

He settled his sunglasses over his eyes. "It's not quite four o'clock, so you're not a year older yet."

The man simply did not forget one detail. He also hadn't forgotten to wear that cologne that drove her to absolute distraction. "Okay, I'm thirty and twenty-three hours, give or take a few minutes. Now let's get this party started. I'm starving." For food and, frankly, a little of his attention.

Kieran drove out of the lot slowly, but the minute he hit the freeway, he turned the car loose. Erica prayed they didn't come upon any serious bottlenecks, or a cop. Not a great way to begin their afternoon.

During the drive, he engaged her in typical small talk about her day, if she'd heard from Stormy, the content of that conversation. After quite a few miles, Erica suddenly realized he was going in the opposite direction from the club. She hated front-seat drivers, but she felt the need to set him straight before they went well out of their way. "I admit I'm directionally challenged, but isn't the club south of the spa?"

"It's technically west, and we're not going to the club."

When he offered no other explanation, she asked, "Don't I deserve a hint?"

"You'll have to wait and see."

She did see something interesting—signs indicating they were on the freeway that led to the coast. "Are we going to Galveston?"

"Yeah, we are. I told you I wanted seafood."

That was certainly the place to find it. "Where are we going to exercise?"

Kieran fired off a grin before turning his attention back to the road. "Have you ever run on the beach?"

Erica's calves began to ache at the thought of slogging through sand. "Actually, no. I've only been to the beach once since I moved to Houston."

"Well, now you're going for a second time."

Fine by her. Except for the sand thing. "Where am I supposed to shower and change before dinner?"

"I've got that handled. Just be patient."

Erica's patience was running on empty when Kieran didn't say much of anything the rest of the way. But not long after they entered the city limits, he pointed to his left. "That's the third location of Bodies By O'Brien," he said. "Or what will be the third location as soon as it's completed next summer."

Erica noticed the site was little more than a shell of a building—a very large building. "If that's where you want me to shower, I'm guessing that involves a water hose since the place clearly has no walls."

"That's not where you're going to shower. Trust me, the particular place I'm taking you has all the amenities you'll ever need."

Good. Now if only she had an inkling where this particular place might be. Maybe a hotel? Not necessarily the case, she decided as they traveled along the boulevard that skirted the seawall, leaving behind the hotels and condos for an area that was much less commercial. After a few more miles, Kieran finally turned right onto a narrow road and left onto another that was dotted with several beachfront properties. When he pulled into the drive of one estate fairly removed from the others in the area, Erica couldn't quite believe what she was seeing. The Gulf of Mexico served as a backdrop for the three-level, gray and white house elevated by several large beams that protected it from rising tides during hurricane conditions. The facade was reminiscent of the Florida plantation homes she'd viewed in magazines, yet it also had several modern architectural details, including arched windows. Lots and lots of windows.

Erica could only gape at Kieran when he pulled up to the garage and shut off the engine. "Are you asking for directions?"

He tossed his shades onto the dash and tugged the keys from the ignition. "No need for that. We're here."

"And where exactly is here?"

"My home away from home."

Surely not… "A weekend rental?"

He opened the door and said, "I own it," then slid out of the car.

Until that moment, Erica hadn't realized the extent of Kieran's wealth. Sure, he had money. The elite car, his successful health clubs and his superior apartment were indicative of that. But she knew the going rate for houses of this caliber—hundreds of thousands of dollars. Perhaps even millions.

She couldn't quite wrap her mind around Kieran as a millionaire. She couldn't imagine what it would be like to own one home, much less two. Especially not one as majestic as this paradise, with its ultramanicured lawns, palm trees and premier landscaping. The front hedge even had a water sculpture. She'd always dreamed of having one of those….

The tap on the window jolted her out of her musings and the car when Kieran opened her door. He grabbed her duffel from the trunk while she took the garment bag and without speaking, they scaled the stairs leading to the front entry.

Kieran opened the elaborate doors to reveal a great room like nothing Erica had ever seen. The interior was decorated with the colors of the ocean—soft blues and sea greens—and a staircase with a chrome banister led to the upper level. The floor plan was wide open, tastefully furnished and absolutely amazing, from the bamboo floors to the plush sofas. Yet the most impressive focal point happened to be the wall of windows that soared all the way to the second floor, revealing a veranda with a boardwalk that led to a private beach.

"My brother-in-law, Whit, designed it. I think he did a fairly good job."

A fairly good job? She turned to find Kieran still standing near the entry. "It's beautiful, but it looks barely lived-in."

He strode into the room and set her bag down next to the sofa. "That's because I don't come here as much as I'd like. But as soon as the new club opens, I plan to make this my permanent home."

A home well over an hour from her house. For all intents and purposes, a world away. "What about your apartment at the club?"

"I'll provide that for the on-site manager as soon as I hire him or her. Of course, if you're interested, we could work something out."

Not unless he came with the package. "Thanks, but no thanks. I prefer living in a house where Stormy has a yard to play in." She draped the garment over the arm of one chair and walked to the windows to view the panorama. "She'd love this set-up, though." And that sounded as if she expected a standing invitation to visit.

"We should bring her out when the weather's warmer."

Maybe that invitation wasn't so far-fetched after all. "I suppose she could practice softball on the beach."

"She could, and speaking of the beach," he said, "are you ready to run?"

She was, but not necessarily on the beach. She had the urge to run from wishing for things that might never come to pass. Still, she faced him with a smile. "Sure. Where do I change?"

He gestured to his left. "In my bedroom."

Finally she'd get to see his bedroom. Regrettably, to check out his decor and nothing more. "How many bedrooms are upstairs?"

"Three, and three baths."

"Are you planning to establish a commune?"

"Yeah, full of fitness rejects, and that's what you'll be if you don't change your clothes so we can jog before nightfall."

If that meant joining his commune, she'd plop her fanny down on the couch and refuse to get up. "All right, Mr. Slave Driver."

After gathering her things, Erica followed Kieran past the equally astounding kitchen with its wraparound bar and stainless-steel appliances that must have cost a fortune.

Good grief, Erica. The whole place cost a fortune.

Give her a few minutes and she'd gladly break in that state-of-the-art stove. But she hadn't come here to play the little wife and cook his meals. She'd come to jog and have some dinner before going back to her own reality.

Yet when she entered the predictably large master suite, she couldn't help but think how incredible it would be to live there. The king-size bed, covered in a steel-gray comforter, was definitely large enough for two with room to spare. Another wall of windows, access to another veranda and, of course, an adjacent exercise area completed the luxurious package.

"The bathroom's to your left," he said. "I'll change in here."

When Erica opened the door, she immediately fell in love with the iron-gray slate tile and granite countertops that complemented the color scheme present in the bedroom. And of all things, a huge whirlpool had been inset into the corner. If she didn't think Kieran would miss her, she'd climb into that tub for a good soak. She might even ask him to join her. Instead, she closed the door and put on a new set of navy warm-ups she'd also purchased, a birthday present for herself, so to speak.

After pulling her hair into a ponytail high atop her head, Erica reentered the bedroom and discovered Kieran had already left the premises. She found him standing on the veranda adjacent to the living room, wearing black shorts and a worn white T-shirt, his back to her as he looked out over the ocean. Such a remarkable view—the placid beach and the buff guy. As far as Erica was concerned, the buff guy with the outstanding butt won out over the beach.

Experiencing a heady jolt of energy, Erica patted Kieran's back on her way down the boardwalk, which she navigated at a full sprint. He caught up to her in a flash and, side by side, they jogged down the beach, past other notable homes belonging to the rich, if not exactly famous.

Even though they didn't speak, Erica enjoyed the comfortable companionship, the freedom she felt as the ocean breeze flowed over her. To bystanders, they would appear to be a couple taking a run together after work. But they weren't exactly a couple, at least not in the traditional sense. Not in the way Erica had begun to secretly desire, in spite of her resolve to avoid impossible scenarios. She had to believe this little escape was only another sign of Kieran's generosity, a way to take her mind off her daughter's absence, the means to keep her from spending a birthday alone. To believe anything else could lead to unrealistic expectations.

After about a mile, Kieran proclaimed they could head back, and when they once again reached the boardwalk, Erica was surprised she wasn't more winded. "That was incredible," she said as they walked back to the house. "More fun than the treadmill."

He forked a hand through his tousled hair. "I like the beach best right after sunrise."

"I'm sure it's beautiful."

"You could see for yourself in the morning."

Had he just suggested she stay overnight? If so, what exactly did that entail in the hours leading up to dawn? Before Erica could question him, Kieran grabbed the hem of his T-shirt.

Don't do it…. Too late.

He whipped the shirt over his head, providing Erica with a private showing of a chest and abdomen she dearly wanted to explore in a very thorough, nonprofessional manner.

"I need a shower," she muttered. A very cold shower even though she doubted that would do a thing to dissolve her wicked thoughts.

"Right this way," Kieran said, and when they arrived back inside, he turned to her with a grin. "We could conserve water and shower together."

The mixed signals had begun to screw with her mind, not to mention what they were doing to her libido. "Isn't that kind of intimate for friends?"

His expression turned suddenly serious. "Is that what we are, Erica? Friends?"

"I'd like to think so. Is that a problem for you?"

"No." He collapsed into a chair and propped his heels on the coffee table. "I just wanted to clarify the ground rules."

"That's right. You're all about the rules."

He frowned. "Meaning?"

"Nothing." She wasn't prepared to get into this now. But later, she wanted answers as to why he'd seemingly altered his attitude about their strictly business relationship.

Back in Kieran's bedroom, Erica withdrew the new outfit from the garment bag, laid it out on the bed and realized she wouldn't be the only one guilty of sending out high-frequency signals tonight, and hers would be sounding loud and clear. The black, barely above-the-knee skirt was innocuous enough, but the silk, turquoise and black print halter top had "do me" written all over it. Okay, maybe that was a bit of a stretch. The bodice did show a good deal of cleavage, but the fabric flowed from an empire waist and ended high on the thigh, adequately covering her hips. She'd also have bare legs and no bra.

Erica could very well face a monumental decision—casual sex with Kieran, or walking away without knowing what she'd missed. But she'd lived far too long in emotional limbo, denying desires that she'd thought had long since died. If she'd learned nothing else from her experiences, she acknowledged life was categorically uncertain and relatively short. If she could have one night with a man whose skills as a lover likely matched his proficiency as a personal trainer, she saw no real reason not to go for it. And that's exactly what she intended to do, if Kieran gave her a sure sign that he wanted the same thing.

Now that she'd made the decision, Erica unclasped the filigree chain holding her wedding band, the one she hadn't removed since the day she'd buried her husband, and stored it inside her makeup case. Another giant step in her quest to regain her confidence and return to the woman she'd once been. A step that could lead to the biggest leap of all—giving herself to another man. If that man was willing to break all the rules.

If Kieran had any doubts where he'd wanted this night to go with Erica, they were all dispelled the minute she joined him in the living room. The fact she wore her hair down was bad enough, but the clothes had the impact of a grenade in Kieran's gut. Nothing better than a silk blouse, particularly one that tied around her neck. Ties were good for easy access…and he was getting way ahead of himself.

Erica sounded a little shaky when she proclaimed, "I'm ready."

So was Kieran—ready to ditch the main course and get

down to dessert. But he had to be patient and respect her wishes. If she wanted to go home tonight, he'd take her. He wouldn't like it, but he'd do it.

She flipped her hair back from her shoulders, allowing him a better view of the whole package. "You look great," he said, and meant it.

She reached up and adjusted his collar. "So do you. I've never seen you in a button-down shirt and slacks before."

He'd never seen her without a bra, either. "Thought it might be a nice change from the usual grunge wear."

She looked around a minute before bringing her gaze back to his. "What's that wonderful smell?"

"Dinner."

"We're not going out?"

He might have made his first mistake of the evening by not making reservations. "Since Friday night usually draws crowds in the local restaurants, especially on a holiday weekend, I decided to have a chef prepare something for us here."

"You have a personal chef?" She looked and sounded astonished.

"You could say that. My sister-in-law, Corri."

"That makes sense," she said. "All the girls at the spa watch her show during afternoon break. She's an incredible chef. But how did you sneak her in here without me knowing it?"

"She came earlier today and cooked everything in advance. And in the hour and a half it took you to get ready, I had plenty of time to take my shower upstairs and heat everything up."

"Sorry. I had to wash—"

"Your hair." And it looked damn good. He imagined it smelled good, too. "I thought we'd eat on the veranda since it's still pretty nice outside."

"That sounds great," she said. "I can't remember the last time I dined outside."

He couldn't recall the last time he'd been this anxious about impressing a woman. Yeah, he could. Never. "Go have a seat. I'll be right out with the food."

Erica walked onto the veranda while Kieran retired to the kitchen. Fortunately, Corri had made it relatively easy for him. She'd put the entrée and vegetables on oven-proof plates, so he only had to heat and serve the food on the patio table that she'd set up for the meal.

When he slid the plate in front of Erica a few minutes later, she frowned. "Is this shrimp scampi?"

Damn, he'd messed up for sure. "You don't like it."

She unfolded her napkin and laid it on her lap. "No. I love it. But it's not the least bit lo-cal."

Kieran pulled a lighter from the pocket in his slacks and lit the candles centered on the table. "Corri made alterations at my request, so it doesn't have the normal high-caloric count."

She smiled. "I appreciate that you thought about me when you planned the meal. In fact, you've thought of everything, haven't you?"

He sure as hell hoped so. "It's not just for you. The only time I stray off course from a healthy diet is once, maybe twice a week, when my mother cooks."

She took a bite and closed her eyes briefly. "This is incredible. Be sure to thank Corri for me."

He'd already thanked Corri both for the meal and her promise not to give any details to Aidan. Of course, his brother would probably attempt to pry it out of her using bedroom tactics, but he sure as hell didn't need to consider anything that might go on in anyone's bedroom. He was having enough trouble ignoring visions of what he wanted to go on in his bedroom with Erica. Watching her eat wasn't helping, either. Every time she took a bite, his attention turned to her mouth.

At this rate, he'd never choke down his own meal, or be able to stand up without risking embarrassment over his lack of control.

Through basic conversation and sheer determination, Kieran willed himself to calm down and managed to eat. Afterward, he cleared the table, refusing Erica's offer of help. He soon returned with chocolate-covered strawberries and a bottle of expensive champagne.

After he doled out the strawberries on two dessert plates and poured the champagne, Erica accepted the glass but waved off the fruit. "Chocolate isn't on my diet."

He pushed the plate toward her. "Like I've said before, Erica, moderation is the key. You can have one or two to satisfy the natural cravings for something sweet."

He had a craving for something sweet right now. And she was sitting across from him.

"I suppose you're right." She bit into one strawberry then closed her eyes briefly. "These are so good, they're sinful."

He'd never seen anyone eat fruit so damn seductively. And when the breeze kicked up, he also noticed she'd begun to develop goosebumps. He could offer her a jacket or take the party back inside. Back inside appeared to be the way to go, he decided, when his gaze wandered to her breasts where he discovered confirmation she was, in fact, cold. And he was getting hotter by the minute.

After picking up the bottle and his glass, he said, "Bring your champagne before you freeze to death and follow me inside." Where he could keep her warm.

Once inside the house, they sat on the floor with their backs to the coffee table, at Erica's request, so they could continue to enjoy the view. Kieran had a great view of her legs where the skirt rode up above her knee. He wanted to explore the terrain with his hands but instead raised his glass for a toast. "Happy Birthday."

She tipped her flute to his. "So far it is a very happy birthday."

When Erica looked wistful, Kieran became concerned. "What are you thinking about?" Hopefully not a quick exit.

"I was just trying to remember the last time I really celebrated my birthday outside of the spa. It was the year after Jeff and I married. He threw a party for me at our campus apartment. We had a really nice time."

One question weighed heavily on Kieran's mind. A question he probably shouldn't ask, but he had to know. "What was your husband like?"

She smiled. "Just your average farm boy. Fairly serious. Old-fashioned."

"How so?"

She sighed. "When Stormy was going through all the surgery, he held down two jobs to make ends meet. I offered to get a part-time job so he could spend some time with the baby, but he believed that Stormy should be my sole focus while he went out and earned the living. Unfortunately, that work ethic resulted in his death."

Kieran briefly debated whether he should stop the conversation now, but he sensed she wanted to talk. "In what way?"

"According to his coworkers, he wasn't paying attention and drove the forklift into some kind of pallets, causing a beam to fall on him."

"Then it happened instantly."

"No. He lived for about an hour. By the time I made it to the hospital, though, it was too late to tell him goodbye. If I didn't have reason enough to hate hospitals after all of Stormy's treatments, I did after that day. I started having panic attacks every time I walked inside one, but I had to work through it for Stormy's sake. Fortunately, I haven't had to worry about that in the past five years."

He couldn't begin to comprehend what she'd faced, but he

admired her that much more after learning the details. "That must've been tough, losing him and having to take care of Stormy by yourself."

"I managed because I had no choice. Thing is, because Jeff was so bent on paying the bills, I had no idea our financial situation was so grim."

"You did get a settlement, right?"

She took a drink of champagne. "Two years later. It was enough to cover the medical bills incurred after Jeff's death, my tuition and to start a small educational trust fund for Stormy. It might have been more if they hadn't considered Jeff at fault. I resented him for not getting enough rest and for not telling me we were so broke. I was angry at him for dying."

A long moment of silence passed before Erica added, "I've never admitted that to anyone. I'm not sure I've ever admitted it to myself."

Kieran draped his arm around her shoulder and pulled her against his side. "Isn't anger one of those phases you talked about on Thanksgiving?"

She ran a fingertip around the rim of the flute. "Yes, but I stayed in that phase longer than I should have. I hated not having someone in my bed at night to tell me that everything was going to be okay. Then one day I realized that I couldn't go on with my life if I stayed angry with him. I finally accepted that no one can prepare for the horrible twists and turns fate sometimes hands you."

He hadn't prepared for her at all. "You're a survivor, Erica. You've also raised a great kid. That's something to be proud of."

She leaned her head against his shoulder. "I am proud of Stormy, but I'm not proud that I let myself go."

He tucked a loose strand of hair behind her ear. "You're working to change that, and doing a damn good job. You look sexy as hell."

Her smile lit up her face. "You think so?"

"Oh, yeah. It's killing me not to touch you the way I really want to touch you. But I'm not going to do that unless I'm sure that's what you want."

She lowered her eyes and toyed with the hem of her skirt. "There wasn't anyone before Jeff, and there hasn't been anyone since."

Information he didn't take lightly. "I'm not going to do anything to hurt you, Erica. I only want to make you feel good."

She centered her gaze on his eyes. "No more worries about what Candice Conrad might say?"

"Unless Candice is hiding out in the closet, she's not going to know what happens between us unless one of us tells her."

"I have a ten o'clock appointment in the morning."

This was the part that could make or break the evening. "I told Joanie that if you're not at the spa by eight-thirty, she's to start canceling your appointments. And I'm willing to throw in a few more training sessions free of charge if you'll agree."

Thankfully, she didn't try to punch him out, but she did say, "I really can't afford to lose the business or the wages."

He hadn't even considered that. "I could loan you the money if you need it." Damn, he sounded almost desperate.

"Wouldn't that make me a paid escort?" she asked in a teasing tone.

Kieran hadn't stopped to consider how his offer might be interpreted in that way. "Sorry. That's not what I intended. I'm just trying to find a way to spend the weekend together without causing you any hardship." He just wanted to be with her that badly.

"The whole weekend, huh?" She threaded her bottom lip between her teeth and looked thoughtful. "I do have only two clients scheduled. One of them is new and one of them never tips. I could make up the pay next week by taking an extra appointment on Tuesday and Wednesday evenings."

Kieran didn't want to pressure her, but he didn't want to leave tonight, either. He brushed a kiss across her forehead, determined to ask one more time before accepting defeat or victory. "Stay with me tonight, Erica. I promise you won't regret it."

Kieran held his breath when Erica didn't immediately answer. He released it slowly when she stood and held out her hands to him. "I'll stay."

Chapter Ten

It had come down to this—those crucial moments following the decision she had made. A decision she couldn't—wouldn't—take back now.

As she followed Kieran past the kitchen, her hand firmly in his, Erica's initial wariness turned into anticipation over what would come next. Her excitement accelerated, along with her pulse, when they entered his bedroom. She reached out to touch his face, to see if he was real, this beautiful man who wanted to be with her—Erica Stevens, a small-town girl who at one time had big dreams. She suspected he would make a few of her secret dreams come true in a matter of minutes.

He lifted her hand, turned it over and kissed her palm. "Have you ever fantasized about making love on a beach?"

She released a tense laugh. "What, and invite sand in places no sand belongs?"

"Don't ruin my attempts at romance," he said, fortunately with a smile.

"Sorry. I haven't had a lot of fantasies in the past few years." Until the day she'd met him.

"What if I bring the beach to us?"

Erica's curiosity climbed. "How do you propose to do that?"

Kieran let her go, walked to the nightstand, picked up a remote control and aimed it at the windows across the lengthy room. With the push of a button, the wall of glass parted, revealing the veranda and the beach beyond. The slight breeze coming off the ocean and the sound of gently lapping waves filtered into the room, creating an ambience that filled Erica with a heady sense of freedom.

She wondered what other magic he had in store for her in the next few moments, though she was already sufficiently under his spell. "Unbelievable," she murmured when he circled his arms around her and pulled her close.

"Let me know if you get too cold," he said. "I have enough heat for both of us."

She didn't doubt that for a moment. "Does the bed do something special, like maybe vibrate?"

"Not unless we're in it, making it vibrate. But we're not going to bed. Yet."

He strode to the closet and returned with several blankets along with a few pillows piled in his arms. "Our own private beach and not a grain of sand in sight," he said as he arranged the bedding on the floor a few feet away from the open windows.

Yes, he'd thought of everything, but Erica guessed he wasn't quite done yet. He confirmed that when he said, "Come here," in a voice so deep and persuasive, she could listen to him for hours on end. But she wanted more than just the sound of his voice. She wanted everything he had to give her.

When Kieran held out his hand, Erica didn't hesitate to go to him. She readily accepted his deep, methodical kiss designed to entice her. And it worked extremely well. By the time they parted, she eagerly waited for him to take her down for the count on the floor beneath her feet. Instead, he tipped his forehead against hers and asked, "Are you nervous?"

Nervous, a little. Excited—very. "You could say that."

"You don't need to be. We're going to go slowly."

Hadn't she heard that from him before? Besides, she wasn't sure she wanted to go slowly. Clearly Kieran had other ideas, she decided, as he knelt down and removed her heels, one at a time. After he skimmed his palms up her legs and brought them to rest immediately beneath her hem, he placed a kiss above each knee. Then he inched the skirt up while Erica looked down on the surreal scene. She fisted her hands at her sides, practically paralyzed from the featherlight touch of his tongue along her inner thighs, first one, and then the other. Yet he didn't travel all that far. At least not as far as she would have liked before he straightened and stood. But the night was still very young, and anything was possible.

After moving her hair aside, he pressed a kiss below her collarbone. "I've wanted to do that all night." He kissed her above her right breast. "And that." He searched for the tie securing her blouse at her neck. "And this, too."

Overcome with a sudden bout of self-consciousness, Erica reached back and clasped his hand before he had the ribbon undone. "Could we turn out the lights, please?"

He presented a wry grin. "I don't see well in the dark."

"And I'm not twenty anymore."

"Twenty-year-olds don't interest me. But if you're more comfortable without the lights, no problem."

Kieran walked to the switch, undoing the buttons on his shirt as he went. The room went dark except for a blue glow from a three-quarter moon reflecting off the water and a series of solar lights lining the boardwalk. When he returned to her, enough illumination still existed for Erica to see his shirt was completely gone. She certainly wasn't nervous now. She was captivated. While he stood quietly watching, she investigated the details of his chest with her fingertips, this time as a woman, not as a therapist. She traced the outline of his biceps, the curve of his shoulders before sliding her palms down his belly, his abdominals contracting at her touch. She switched her focus to his back for the time being, and followed the track of his spine down to his remarkable butt. She wanted to know that territory without the constraints of clothing, but it seemed Kieran was bent on removing her clothes first.

When she felt the release of her skirt's clasp and the downward track of the zipper, she shivered slightly. When the fabric slid down her legs to the floor to join her shoes, she started to shake.

"Are you cold?" Kieran whispered, his breath warm and soft against her ear.

She stepped out of the skirt and nudged it aside with her foot. "Just the opposite."

"Good." Leaving one hand on her waist, he fished through his pocket with the other and withdrew a condom that he tossed onto the makeshift beach.

He again tugged on the tie at her neck. "Mind if I take care of this now?"

Erica could only nod as he released the ribbon, causing the bodice to fall. Then he simply stood there and studied her before a smile gradually appeared. "You're beautiful."

She'd never considered herself beautiful before, but Kieran's assurances could convince her otherwise, at least for tonight, while the lights were dim.

Kieran pulled the blouse over her head and tossed it over

his shoulder. Aside from her panties, she was now totally bare to his eyes, bare for his touch. Yet he didn't touch her. He did take a seat in a nearby chair to remove his shoes and socks, all the while keeping an eye on her, as if sizing her up. She wanted to cover herself at first, but the more he looked, the more she wanted him to look. If he found her lacking, he certainly didn't show it. On the contrary, he came back to her quickly and his subsequent kiss was longer than the last. More suggestive than the last.

After a time, he stepped back, his hand poised on his fly. "Have you changed your mind?"

"No." Even that simple word took great effort.

And then the slow part kicked back in, when Kieran began to remove his slacks and briefs. She questioned if he was taunting her, or perhaps giving her another chance to reconsider. But how on earth could she when he stood there, completely nude and unmistakably wanting her?

He only allowed her a few moments to look before he brought her down on the blanket in his arms, her panties the only barrier between them. But he disposed of those swiftly, leaving more soft kisses in their wake before he worked his way back up her body. Erica dearly wanted to touch him and as if he'd read her mind, he turned her to face him, laid her palm against his chest, then slowly, slowly moved it downward. Down his ridged abdomen. Down past the slight indentation of his navel. Down to the final destination. Such a long time, she thought as she investigated the nuances with curious and careful hands. Such a long time since she'd enjoyed the feel of a man, the sound of his ragged breathing when she explored without hesitation, the tension in his body when she'd pushed him to the edge.

"That's enough," Kieran muttered as he clasped her wrist and brought her palm back against his chest. "Your hands are one of your best features. But only one of the best."

When Kieran nudged her onto her back and closed his mouth over her breast, Erica's entire body reacted to the pull of his lips, the circular motion of his tongue. Even the breeze streaming in from outside didn't alleviate the heat resulting from a need that had been dormant for a very long time. An odd, throaty sound escaped from her lips and that might have embarrassed her had Kieran not responded by guiding his hand between her thighs.

She welcomed the sensations incited by his deliberate yet gentle touch, but it took only a matter of moments before the pressure rapidly escalated and a forceful climax took hold. She was lost in the incredible pleasure until awareness and unease settled over her. "I'm sorry," she said when Kieran leveled his gaze on her. "It's been a long time."

He kissed her softly. "No apology necessary. There's plenty more where that came from."

In the minutes that followed, Kieran proved that to be true, with his hands, with his mouth, with sensual words of encouragement. Erica was amazed by his skill, by her own body's response, the absolute euphoria that went straight to her head. And by the time he finally slipped into her body, she was on the verge of tears.

Erica refused to cry, and she didn't while Kieran moved inside her, his power and control apparent with every deep thrust. She couldn't think when the next climax she hadn't contemplated arrived with a vengeance. After she recovered, she thought of nothing more than the sensory details—his damp skin and the flex of his muscles beneath her hands. The way his respiration picked up cadence, harder and harder, right before he shuddered, then stilled against her. She truly valued these aftermath moments, the feel of his weight, the sound of his satisfied sigh, the knowledge that he'd gained as much gratification as she had. She realized then how much she had missed over the years, how she hadn't even allowed herself to imagine this intimacy with another living soul. How close she felt to him at that moment, in spite of the possible risk to her heart.

After a few more moments, Kieran released a long groan before he rolled to his back, taking her with him. And when she glimpsed that wonderful smile, the one he always gave her when she'd done something right, the tears she'd tried so hard to retain fell against his chest.

His smile faded and concern took its place. "I didn't hurt you, did I?"

She swiped her fingertips over her damp eyes. "They're not those kind of tears, and I'm not sad." How could she explain what he had done for her? She could only try and hope that he understood. "For the first time in a very long time, I finally feel whole and alive again."

All the ways he'd given her pleasure, all the proof he'd provided that he was the consummate lover, paled in comparison to what Kieran O'Brien—the tough guy with the heart of gold and the strength of a hundred men—did next. He took her in his arms, smoothed his hands over her hair and whispered, "You're going to be okay."

"Are you awake?"

Kieran opened his eyes to find Erica seated beside him on the edge of the bed, coffee cup in hand. She was fresh faced, wide-awake and fully clothed, while he was half-asleep, practically dead to the world and buck naked. He had her to thank for that. All of it. Of course, he could have taken her home the day before and saved some of his strength. He could have kept his hands off her the previous two nights, and most of yesterday, but he hadn't. In fact, he wanted his hands on her now, and he wanted her naked again.

"What day is it?"

"It's Sunday, and I was beginning to think you weren't going to get up."

He rolled to his back and stacked his hands behind his head. "In case you haven't noticed, I'm already up."

Her gaze shot to his groin before she nailed him with a sultry look. "I see that, but before you get any ideas, remember I have to pick up my child in a few hours."

"True." He'd almost forgotten about Stormy's return to Houston. Then again, his thoughts had been centered on Stormy's mother. "Where have you been?"

"I went for a run on the beach."

He glanced at the clock to discover it was close to noon. He hadn't slept this late since college. "Why didn't you wake me? I would've gone with you."

"I tried," she said as she set the cup down on the nightstand. "You wouldn't budge."

"That's because you put me in a sex-induced coma."

She playfully slapped at his exposed rib cage. "I don't recall you issuing any protests."

"And I didn't know you were so deceptive. Behind those dimples and that farm-girl face resides a damn wicked woman."

She stretched out on top of him and rested her chin on his chest. "You've only scratched the surface, O'Brien."

Oh, yeah, he figured as much. Unfortunately, they were down to the last condom and running out of time. And he needed what time they had left to include an honest discussion. On that thought, he kissed her forehead and told her, "Before I do any more surface scratching, we need to talk."

She looked worried. Extremely worried. "What's this about?"

"If you'll let me put some clothes on, I'll tell you."

After Erica stood, Kieran climbed from the bed, retrieved

a pair of pajama bottoms from the bureau and slipped them on. He turned to find Erica standing as stiff as the headboard. What he had to say to her wouldn't be easy, but he couldn't leave here without getting some things out in the open.

He sat on the edge of the mattress and patted the spot beside him. "Sit." She did, slowly. "First of all," he said, "I'm resigning as your personal trainer."

"But—"

"I'm not abandoning you. I'm going to have Evie take over your program, which means I'll still be helping you unofficially."

"I don't understand." Her expression made that perfectly clear.

Because he frankly sucked at true confessions, he took a second to prepare to tell her exactly how he felt. To say what he should have said to her last night, when he talked to her about a hell of a lot of things he'd never discussed with any other women, including his sour relationship with his twin. She'd listened to him then. He hoped she listened to him now.

"I've had two long-term relationships, but neither worked out," he began. "I even came close to being engaged about a year ago, before that relationship went south. I'm not a saint, but I'm not a player, either. Once I commit to someone, I commit completely. And I want to commit to this relationship with you. I realize there aren't any guarantees it will work, but I want to try it, if you're willing."

Either she was in shock, or still struggling to absorb his suggestion, because it took a few moments before she asked, "Do you mean you and me, as a couple?"

"Yeah, that's what I mean."

"Dating?"

"That's usually what couples do." He took her hands into

his. "You don't have to decide right now. I needed you to know that I care about you and I want to be with you beyond this weekend."

She came to her feet and paced a few times before returning to stand before him. "This isn't just the great sex talking, is it?"

It wasn't about the sex. It hadn't been from the day he'd met her.

He grabbed her hand and tugged her forward between his parted knees. "I consider the sex a perk, your smart mouth a challenge and your courage unbelievable. Your kid's pretty great, too."

She pressed her hand to her mouth, her eyes wide. "If we do this, I'll have to tell Stormy."

"Do you think she's going to care?"

"I know she won't because I asked her." Color spread over her cheeks. "Not about you specifically, of course. I asked her if she'd mind if I dated someone, and she said no, as long as it was someone like you."

Smart kid. "Good. Since that's resolved, what do you say? Do we see each other outside the gym? Or do we continue the way we've been, fighting our attraction to each other until we're both half-insane?"

Finally, she smiled. "We know that doesn't work." She studied the ceiling for a moment before bringing her gaze back to him. "I guess my answer is, why not? I can't think of anything better to do."

Overcome by a strong sense of satisfaction, he fell back onto the bed, pulling her down on top of him. "How about we both get naked and get wicked?"

"We don't have a lot of time and we still need to shower."

He kissed her hard and quick, before setting them both back on their feet. "Then let's go conserve some water."

* * *

She felt as if she'd been on a nonstop thrill ride since she'd left work on Friday. The thought that Kieran wanted more than only a weekend kept the butterflies stirring in Erica's belly, all the way to the airport and back home again. Stormy had talked incessantly most of the trip, until she'd fallen asleep, totally unaware when Kieran carried her into the house and laid her on the bed.

Erica stood in the doorway and watched Kieran remove her daughter's shoes and cover her with the throw from the end of the bed before he shut off the lamp. He was going to make an excellent father and husband, a thought that caused her to take a mental step back. She saw no good reason to start picket-fence dreaming only hours after their decision to pursue a relationship. In fact, she decided not to mention anything to Stormy for at least another few days. Why, she couldn't say. Maybe she still didn't quite believe it herself. Maybe she feared Kieran might change his mind once the weekend excitement evaporated. Maybe she was being too cautious, but she'd rather err on that side than have to let her daughter down later. Yet when he met her at the door, slipped his arm around her waist and walked her down the hallway, she couldn't quell her wishful thinking.

After they reached the living room, he brought her fully into his arms and kissed her softly. "Think she's out for the night?"

"It's still fairly early, so I wouldn't be surprised if she woke up in an hour or two."

"That's too bad."

Erica knew what he was thinking—she'd been thinking it, too. But having Kieran spend the night wasn't a good idea. "Before you try to whisk me away into the bedroom, and believe me that normally wouldn't bother me, I don't want to risk Stormy finding out about us before I have a chance to talk to her. Not to mention she's at an impressionable age."

"You're right," he said, a hint of disappointment in his voice. "Finding time to be alone could be tough."

"That's what sleepovers are for."

He grinned. "And surrogate grandparents, which reminds me. You should know up front what being an O'Brien girlfriend entails."

Erica couldn't help but laugh. "I'm sorry. That whole girlfriend thing sounds so strange to me, especially at my age."

"I think it's better than referring to you as my lover, especially in front of my mother."

"True. Girlfriend it is." Which made him her boyfriend. She'd never thought she'd have one of those again.

"Anyway," he continued. "You'll have an open invitation to Sunday lunch and any other get-togethers that might occur, including the holidays. But then you'll probably want to spend Christmas with your folks, and that's okay."

Talk of family gatherings and holidays gave Erica a fuzzy feeling inside. "Actually, I just learned that my parents are spending the holiday with my brother and his new girlfriend in Seattle this year."

"That settles it then. You and Stormy can come with me to Mom and Dad's. A word of warning, though. My mother really gets into the whole holiday thing. She cooks most of the week before."

Erica had only celebrated in the past for Stormy's sake. This year she might have something solid to celebrate, namely finding a man who had strong values and an equally strong support system. But that was still a month away, and anything could happen in a month. "Speaking of cooking, I could make some dinner for us, if you're hungry."

He had that "I'm starving" look in his eye, but not necessarily for food. "No thanks. I'm going to go home now and let you catch up on your sleep."

"Are you sure you don't want to hang around awhile longer?"

"Yeah, I do, and that's why I need to leave. Otherwise, I can't be responsible for my actions because right now, making out with you in the Porsche is starting to sound real good."

Making out and boyfriends. She felt like a teenager again. "That's sounds tempting, but with my luck, we'd get caught. Maybe we should try it some other time."

He bent and ran kisses along her jaw. "We still have a lot to try."

After all they'd done this past weekend, she had a hard time believing they hadn't covered most everything. Then again, this was Kieran, who'd had no qualms about guiding her into a level of intimacy she'd never before experienced. And if she kept thinking about that, she could find herself playing backseat bingo without regard to common decency and her advanced age. "As much as I hate for you to go, I do have a few things to do to get ready for work tomorrow and you'll only distract me."

He grinned. "Are you going to write about us in your diary?"

He wished—and she was. "Yes. I'm going to record how I became a human pretzel at the hands of a tremendously creative lover."

"Like my dad once said, those gymnasts are a flexible lot. You definitely proved that to me in the shower earlier."

This kind of talk had gotten them into trouble before. If Erica didn't encourage his departure, they could propel past that no-return point in record time. "Get out now before I call Lucy and tell her you're being a bad boy."

"She'd never believe it, and I'm going."

But he didn't go until he had kissed her back to the

boneless stage, where she'd been almost all of the past forty-eight hours. Kieran's cell phone served as a somewhat timely interruption, although he didn't seem to appreciate that at all, apparent by his irritable greeting. And although she couldn't discern the content of the conversation, she did sense something wasn't quite right.

After saying, "I'll be there in a few minutes," Kieran flipped the phone closed and shoved it back into his hip pocket. "That was my brother Devin, the doctor. He asked me to stop by the hospital on the way home because he has some serious issue he needs to discuss with me."

Erica's heart began to beat erratically the minute she heard *hospital.* "Is something wrong with one of the family?"

"He didn't provide any details." He planted a quick kiss on her lips. "I'll call you tomorrow morning."

Erica followed him to the door, and when he stepped on the porch, she said, "I hope everything's okay."

"It could be just another baby on the way." He attempted a smile that fell short of fully forming. "It's probably nothing."

He'd never seen his brother look so serious, although when in doctor mode, Devin was always serious. But not to this degree.

The leather chair Kieran sat in across from Devin's desk was growing less comfortable by the minute, mostly due to his brother's silence. And he couldn't stand the suspense any longer. "Just spill it, Dev."

After picking up a folder, Devin cleared his throat. "What I'm about to tell you now isn't pleasant. In fact, it's the worst thing we've faced as a family."

Kieran's imagination began to take several turns, none of which were good. "Is something wrong with Dad?"

"No. It's Kevin. He's seriously ill."

Of all the family members Devin could have named, Kevin would have been the last on Kieran's list of possibilities. Granted, his twin lived in the fast lane, but he hadn't been sick a day since childhood. Then he remembered Kevin's appearance last Thursday. The signs that he'd chalked up to a hangover. "What's wrong with him?"

Devin opened the folder. "He has idiopathic aplastic anemia, which means his bone marrow has stopped making new blood cells. It has no known cause."

Kieran's mind reeled from the possibilities, one in particular that he immediately rejected. "What are they doing to treat this?"

"For the past few months, he's been undergoing transfusions under the care of a hematologist."

"For the past few *months?* Why the hell hasn't he told anyone?"

"He didn't want anyone to worry, especially Mom."

Understandable considering how she'd always fretted over Kevin, whether he needed it or not. "And these transfusions are helping him?"

"They're sustaining him," Devin said. "But they won't for much longer."

"I'm not understanding any of this, Dev."

He looked away for a minute before returning his grim gaze back to Kieran. "It's not good."

Unable to sit still any longer, Kieran shot to his feet. "I don't know what the hell you're saying, Devin, but I want you to just say it!"

Devin's hesitation was telling, the silence deafening, the truth unbelievable.

"Kevin's dying."

Chapter Eleven

In that moment, Kieran felt as if he'd stepped into a never-ending nightmare, the kind that wouldn't let go, even long after you awakened. The strength he'd always coveted seeped away and he dropped back into the chair. No matter how angry he'd been with Kevin over the years, he couldn't stop the sadness. He couldn't accept the diagnosis, either. "In this day and age, are you telling me there's no cure?"

Devin leaned back in the chair and streaked a palm over his jaw. "Actually, there is a possible cure, and that's where you come in. Kevin needs a bone-marrow transplant, and since you're identical twins, you have the same antigens. That makes you the ideal marrow donor."

"And it's a guaranteed fix?"

"About a seventy-percent chance, barring complications. The process before the transplant can be dangerous. Kevin will have to be admitted into a transplant unit where he'll receive medications and undergo chemotherapy to destroy his own marrow in preparation to receive yours."

Chemotherapy, bone-marrow transplants—words Kieran had never thought much about until now. "What would I have to do procedure-wise?"

"The extraction takes place in an O.R. under general anesthesia. You'll have a few puncture marks in the back around your pelvic bone. Knowing you, you'll be back to your routine in a few days, a month at the longest. About the only real risk would be if you react badly to the anesthesia."

Luckily, he'd already been through the rigors of knee surgery without incident. "And this is Kevin's only alternative?"

"It's the only hope we have of saving him. If you don't want to do it, any of the siblings can be tested to see if they're a close match, but that carries a greater risk of rejection. You're Kevin's best option."

Once again, he found himself in the position of saving Kevin, only this time he'd literally be saving his life. "Why isn't Kevin here talking to me?"

"He didn't want to ask you because he doesn't think you'll agree."

Kieran wondered how the rift between them had grown so wide that Kevin honestly believed he wouldn't step up to the plate. "I'll do it. Just let me know where I need to be and when."

Devin looked more than a little relieved. "Great. I'll have someone at the center give you a call and set everything up. You'll start by having routine blood work and a physical in the next couple of days. We have to move fast before Kevin gets worse. There's one more thing you need to know."

Kieran wasn't sure how much more he could handle. "Shoot."

"This is going to be tough on Kevin, before and after the transplant. He'll be in isolation for a few weeks after he receives the marrow, so it's important he has a lot of emotional support before the transplant. Since he doesn't want anyone else to know right now, that means the responsibility falls on us. I'll see him when I can, but with my schedule and the family obligations, it's going to be rough."

And that meant Kieran would shoulder most of the burden of keeping his brother's spirits as elevated as possible. That in itself could be the greatest challenge of all. "He has to tell Mom and Dad at some point in time."

"True, but I agree with Kevin. It might be better if we wait until closer to the time for the procedure since we both know how Mom worries about him, even when she doesn't have a damn thing to worry about."

This time, though, she would have something to worry about. "When will they do the transplant?"

"In about two weeks, so you'll have enough time to recover before the holidays."

Like he really cared about the holidays in light of this sorry news. Kieran's only concern centered around getting out of there so he could think. On that note, he came to his feet and fished his keys from his pocket. "Just let me know when Kevin's admitted and I'll stop by to see him."

"I will." Devin rose and tapped the folder on the desktop. "This isn't going to be easy on you, either, Kieran. Call me if you need anything, even if it's only to talk. Better still, talk to Erica. I know you were with her this weekend."

Kieran didn't bother to question how Devin knew; word spread like wildfire in the O'Brien clan. "I can't involve her in this. She's been through too much already."

"That's your decision," Devin said. "I only know that when I come home after a bad day at the hospital, talking to Stacy is the only thing that keeps me sane. This habit you have of keeping all your emotions bottled up for everyone else's sake is going to shave years off your life."

Kieran didn't have the strength to argue. "I'll be fine. I'll see you later."

After he strode out of the hospital and settled into the Porsche, the anger came rushing in with the force of an explosion. Anger over the circumstances. Anger over the lack of control. Anger over the timing. He owned enough fury to punch a hole in the windshield but instead pounded his palm against the steering wheel three times in rapid succession.

He wanted like hell to see Erica, but he couldn't see her, not for a while. He couldn't throw her into the middle of a medical crisis. He couldn't ask her to be there when he underwent the procedure, either, even if that procedure carried minimal risk. But he wasn't naive enough to think that life came with automatic guarantees—what he'd learned tonight was proof positive of that—and asking her to subject herself to a hospital vigil for his sake would be totally unfair to her.

Besides, Kevin needed his attention right now, which meant he'd have to devote most of his time to mending those proverbial fences. If he didn't take care of that now, he could be facing a lifetime of regret if, God forbid, he couldn't save Kevin this time.

Until this waking nightmare ended, he'd be no good to Erica. He couldn't give her his time and he couldn't give her any real stability. He couldn't give her any promises that everything would be okay because he wasn't sure it would.

But he had to be strong for his family and for Kevin. He wouldn't let anyone see how this was tearing him up inside, not even Erica. Especially not Erica.

"Mom, you're going too fast!"

Realizing she was practically dragging Stormy across the health club's parking lot, Erica slowed her steps. "I'm sorry, sweetie. I'm just trying to catch up with Kieran before he leaves." And he was going to leave in twenty minutes, something she'd learned from the receptionist when she'd called.

"How come Kieran hasn't been around all week?" Stormy asked.

Precisely Erica's question, and the reason why she was there. He'd only called once since their return from Galveston, and that was just to say she should come in and work out with Evie, and he'd be tied up all week. She'd sensed something was wrong, but he refused to talk at length. Well, that was about to come to an end. She wanted answers, and she wanted them now.

When they stepped inside the club, Erica took Stormy by the shoulders. "Go into the playroom and finish your homework. This shouldn't take long."

"I want to see Kieran."

"You can't right now, sweetie. But I'll tell him you asked about him."

Backpack in hand, Stormy huffed off and Erica crossed the gym, heading straight for Kieran's sanctuary. She didn't wave at the front-desk personnel, didn't stop to talk with her latest trainer and she didn't hesitate to walk into his office without knocking. He wasn't at his desk, but she did find him in the private gym, stretched out on the weight bench, pumping iron with a vengeance. When he caught sight of her, he dropped the barbell onto the bracket and sat up. For a split second he looked as if he might be glad to see her. But he disproved that theory when he asked, "What are you doing here?" as if he didn't welcome her unexpected visit.

Erica's anger began to bubble near the boiling point. "Nice to see you, too. And I'm here because I haven't heard a thing from you since Monday night."

"I told you I was going to be tied up."

"Yes, and that's all you said. It's what you didn't say that's bothering me."

He frowned. "I don't know what you're getting at."

Maybe not, but he would. "If you've reconsidered our relationship, just say so. I'm not going to fall apart. But if that is the case, I wish you would have told me so after our weekend. I would've preferred 'I had a nice time, see you around' than all your talk about family holidays and dating."

He came to his feet, grabbed a towel and swiped it across his damp forehead. "This isn't about us."

She crossed her arms over her middle. "Maybe not, but what am I supposed to think unless you tell me what's going on with you?"

Unmistakable turmoil brewed in his dark eyes. "Trust me, you don't want to know what's going on."

"Yes, I do. Anything's better than not knowing."

"I can't talk about it now."

"Can't or won't? I realize I tend to talk a lot, but I'm also a good listener. And you look like you need that right now."

"I'm okay," he said without much conviction. "This involves a family matter, and it's not something you need to worry about."

She bristled at the same admonishment she'd heard from Jeff on several occasions. "Does it have something to do with Kevin?"

Erica saw a spark of acknowledgment in his expression before his face once more turned into a noncommittal mask. "Yeah. He's in serious trouble."

"And it's your responsibility to rescue him again."

He leaned a shoulder against the treadmill. "This is different."

"How is it different?"

"Look, Erica, it's my problem, not yours. My parents don't even know about it yet. You've come a long way with your fitness program. You need to concentrate on that and let me handle this issue."

She hated his dismissal as much as she hated having this conversation. "I don't intend to go back to my old habits, so that's one less thing you need to worry about."

"I'm sure you won't."

Erica wasn't getting through that impenetrable wall he'd built around himself, but she wasn't ready to give up yet. "I'm about to take Stormy home. I'll be up later if you change your mind and want to talk about this."

"I need to handle this in my own way."

"And your way is to take it all on yourself." She hugged her arms tighter to her middle. "Does it ever get tiring, carrying everyone else's burden on your shoulders?"

"I'm only trying to protect you, Erica. This isn't a good situation. I'm not sure you can han—" His gaze wandered away.

"I see." And she did, all too clearly. "You were going to say you didn't think I could handle it. Now you're treating me exactly like Jeff used to treat me. In fact, you're acting like him. He thought it was a sign of weakness to show any vulnerability. I never knew if he was sad or angry or scared when Stormy was sick. I didn't know what he was feeling most of the time, and that's no way to sustain a relationship. I refuse to subject myself to that again."

"What are you saying?"

"I'm saying that relationships are about give and take, sharing the good and the bad, not bearing all the burden because you think anything else makes you less of a man." When she saw a flicker of response, she believed she'd hit on something important. "Is that what happened to your other relationships, Kieran? You refused to let your guard down even for a minute?"

He tossed the towel to the ground and ran a hand over his nape. "I can't deal with this right now, Erica. But after this is over, we'll talk about it then."

"In a week? A month? When you're good and ready?" As badly as she hated what she was about to say, she still had to say it. "Don't bother, Kieran. I don't see any reason to discuss it further. You're obviously not ready to have a real relationship."

Now he looked stunned. "That's it? You're going to just give up on us?"

She didn't want to, but she saw no choice. "Stormy's starting to rely on you, and she's already lost one important man in her life. I understand that relationships don't come with guarantees, but if you're not willing to give ours your all, then it's best if we end it now, before she believes there's more between us than friendship."

"I don't want to be just your friend." He took a step toward her then stopped, as if he wanted to touch her but decided it wouldn't be best. "I want to make this work, Erica. I swear to God, I do."

"It won't work if you shut me out at the first sign of trouble because you don't think I'm equipped to handle bad news, or because you have this need to take care of every problem by yourself. Last weekend I told you things I've never told anyone because I trusted you. I expect you to trust me enough to do the same."

When he didn't speak, she continued. "In a perfect world, nothing bad would ever happen. But bad things do happen, Kieran, and learning to rely on the people who care about you is sometimes the only thing that can get you through those times. If you can't learn to do that, then you're never going to have a meaningful relationship, unless you find someone who doesn't care how you feel. But I do care about you." More than he knew. More than she should.

He sighed. "I care about you, too, Erica. That's why this is so damn unfair."

At least that was something. "If that's true, then you'll

think long and hard about what I've said. If you can't give me what I need—and what I need is someone who gives me more than a pat on the head and a 'don't worry, I'll handle it'—then I wish you the best of everything."

Before the tears began to flow, Erica turned around and marched out of the office. She had to hold it together until she had Stormy safely home and in bed. Then she would have a good cry.

Erica retrieved Stormy from the playroom and didn't say much of anything until they were in the car. "Did you finish your homework?" she asked as they pulled out of the lot.

"Yeah. Did you make Kieran mad?"

Probably so. "Why do you think that?"

"Because he's not training you anymore. And because he's not coming over like he used to. What about my softball, Mom? Is he going to help me?"

Erica didn't have any good answer to give her child, and she hated that. "Kieran's taking care of a family problem right now. I'll see if we can find someone else to help you in the meantime. Maybe a high school girl." She sent a quick glance at Stormy. "You'd like that, wouldn't you?"

Stormy gave her a quelling look. "I don't want a high school girl. I want Kieran to help me, or his sister."

"I'm sorry, Stormy, but sometimes we don't get what we want." She'd learned that hard lesson a few minutes ago.

The conversation ceased until halfway home when Stormy asked, "Are we ever going to be a real family, Mom?"

Erica had always been primed for the questions about Jeff, about kissing and sex and growing up. But she hadn't prepared for this. "We are a real family, sweetie."

"I mean am I ever going to have another dad?"

More questions without concrete answers. "I just don't know, Stormy. I just don't know."

* * *

"Don't you have somewhere else to be?"

Kieran looked up from his cards to Kevin, who'd been drifting in and out of sleep for the past hour. His brother looked like hell. He'd been through hell. "I'm making sure you don't escape before the procedure tomorrow."

"Like I really have the strength to go anywhere." He took a drink of water from the cup resting on the rolling tray positioned between them. "But come to think of it, we could play one of our old switch-the-twin tricks. I'll yank this tube out of my chest, go have a beer and you can take my place until they realize you're not me."

In some ways, Kieran wished he could take his brother's place. "No way. That would require me cutting my hair, and I'm already giving you my bone marrow."

Kevin leaned his head back on the pillow and stared at the ceiling. "I've been thinking about that marrow thing." He turned his head toward Kieran and narrowed his eyes. "Does this mean I'm going to want to go to the gym seven days a week instead of five and start craving soy?"

"I don't eat soy." Kieran glanced at the clock suspended on the wall above the TV. "It's getting late. I thought Mom and Dad were coming by."

"I told them I'd see them tomorrow. Mom already spent most of the day with me. If she asked me one more time how I was feeling, I would've broken out of this cell and taken my chances."

He could understand where Kevin was coming from in that regard. Lucy hadn't taken the illness news well, although she was her usual optimistic self, or at least she was putting up a good front. "Where's your new girlfriend?"

Kevin closed his eyes briefly before opening them again. "Leah?"

"Is she the pediatrician?"

"Yeah," Kevin said. "She went home to Mississippi a couple of months ago. She's supposed to be back in the spring to finish her fellowship before she goes into private practice."

"Sounds like she's one smart lady."

"Yeah, she's smart, and don't look so surprised."

"But I'm betting she's blond."

Kevin shot him a dirty look. "Brunette. She's great. Beautiful. More important, she knows all my faults, but that didn't seem to matter."

That had to be a first for his twin. "Sounds like the real deal."

"It might have been, but I'll never know. It ended right after my diagnosis."

Kieran wondered why she sounded too good to be true. "You mean she left you because you're sick?"

"I broke it off without telling her. I didn't know what was going to happen, and I couldn't put her through that."

This was starting to sound all too familiar to Kieran. "She's a doctor, Kev. She'd understand."

"More than most people, but I couldn't commit to her knowing this thing could kill me. And for the first time, I did want to commit to a woman." Kevin sent him a wry grin. "Maybe this is my punishment for all the mistakes I've made over the years."

His brother had made a lot of mistakes, but Kevin didn't deserve this. "You're going to get through this. And after you do, it's not too late to give her a call and explain it to her."

"It wouldn't be fair, Kieran. She grew up in a family with parents who took in foster kids, which is why she became a pediatrician. She wants kids of her own, too, and after undergoing the chemo, I have a fifty-fifty chance of being sterile."

Damn. That was something Devin failed to mention during their initial conversation about Kevin's disease. "You're an

O'Brien male. The odds are good you'll end up on the right side of the fifty percent. We have strong swimmers."

Kevin didn't appear to appreciate his attempt at lightening the mood. "I won't know that for a while. And even if I do get out of this with both my life and sterility intact, then it's still too late for me to make amends with Leah. I don't think she was too happy with my usual 'I'm not looking to settle down' speech."

"It's never too late to correct a mistake." Like he was one to hand out advice he couldn't seem to follow.

Kevin nailed him with a questioning look. "What about you and Erica? I haven't heard you mention her."

For the past two weeks, Erica had been all he'd thought about. He really didn't want to get into that, but since Kevin had been honest with him, he might as well return the favor. "It's over between us, although I didn't want it to be over."

"Both of us screwed up for a change?" Kevin laughed. "That's rich."

Kieran leaned back in his chair and focused on the tile floor. "Problem is, I didn't realize I was screwing up. When I decided not to tell her about this ordeal, I was trying to protect her. She lost her husband, she had a sick kid and I didn't want to put her through anything remotely resembling a medical issue. She said my need to protect everyone alienates the people I care about."

"She's right." When Kieran's gaze snapped to Kevin, his brother held up his hands. "Before you coldcock me, hear me out."

Kieran wasn't in the mood for any criticism. "I don't need a speech."

"Shut up and listen." Kevin scooted up on the bed and looked at him straight on. "I honestly didn't mind you fighting my battles when we were kids and I was too scrawny to defend myself. But when I got older and bigger, it got on my nerves. You tried to make up for my shortcomings by always walking the straight line. But the straighter the line, the more I veered off course. Between Mother thinking I could do no wrong, and you thinking I couldn't do anything right, I went on a thirty-year rebellion. And it took Leah pointing that out to me before I finally got it."

"I thought she was a pediatrician, not a damn psychologist."

"I told you she's smart. And just because I gave up the best thing that's ever happened to me, that doesn't mean you should follow my lead. Go talk to Erica and make it right."

For once, his brother was making sense. "I'm not sure she'll see me."

"You won't know until you try, and you need to try before more time passes. Believe me, it's lonely down here at the bottom."

Kevin was right—he still had the opportunity to set things straight with Erica and convince her that he was going to try to do the honorable thing by her and Stormy. Otherwise, he'd be losing the best thing he ever had.

Kieran quickly pushed out of the chair, more than ready to head to Erica's house. "Guess the next time I see you, you'll be asking for sprouts with your lunch."

Kevin grinned. "Get out of here."

On the way to the door, Kieran paused and faced Kevin again. He wanted to thank him for pointing out that life was too short to put things off until it was too late, but Kevin had already fallen back to sleep. For the first time in years, Kieran felt as if they'd gained solid ground toward reconciliation. He hoped the same held true with Erica.

Chapter Twelve

Thursday pizza night had become a thing of the past, making way for birthday sleepovers and best friends. Erica had realized that all too well when she'd dropped Stormy off at Lisa's a half hour ago for a birthday and school holiday celebration. Now she sat alone in the den with only her thoughts of Kieran for company. The silence was so stark that when the doorbell rang, she physically jumped. She wondered if Stormy had decided to come home. A ridiculous assumption. Her daughter had better things to do than sit with a mother who'd come down with a solid case of self-pity.

Erica pushed off the sofa and walked to the door to peer through the peephole. And as it had been all those weeks ago, she discovered Kieran standing on the threshold, as if she'd somehow conjured him up. He looked tired, but good. Too good. She had no clue why he was there. More important, she had no idea what to say.

This is not that difficult, Erica. She finally gathered the wherewithal to open the door and the strength to step onto the porch to face him. "Hi." A simple greeting, but the only thing she could think of at the moment.

He held up a pink gift bag. "Stormy's birthday present."

She was impressed he'd remembered, and admittedly disappointed he hadn't come to see her. "Unfortunately, she's at Lisa's for the night."

He offered her the bag. "Give it to her for me. It's a new ball glove."

She took the bag and held it against her. "She'll love it."

He leaned a shoulder against the porch's support and studied her a moment. "You cut your hair."

Erica's hand immediately went to where her hair touched her shoulders. "I needed a change." She no longer needed to hide behind it.

"It looks great." A few moments of silence passed before he added, "I've been thinking a lot about what you said at the club that night. You were right. I'm damn bad at talking about my feelings. But I'd like to try, if that's okay."

Erica tried hard not to hope, but a part of her couldn't help it. "I'm listening."

"First of all," he began, "that weekend in Galveston, when we talked about my problems with Kevin and how hard it was to give up baseball, I told you more than I've ever told any woman. It might seem like surface stuff to you, but it was a big step for me. I hope you know that."

"I do now." She also knew he was still troubled. "How is Kevin?"

He drew in a deep breath and let it out slowly. "He's sick, and he has been for several months. He didn't tell anyone until he found out he was dying."

Erica bit back a gasp over the terrible revelation and the

abject pain in his expression. "I'm so sorry, Kieran. I wish you would have said something. No one knows better than me what you're going through."

"Which is why I should have told you from the beginning. When I said you couldn't handle it, that was only an excuse. The truth is, I couldn't handle it. Hell, I didn't want to believe it."

She intimately understood everything he was feeling. Every raw emotion, especially the disbelief. "Can anything be done for him?"

He kicked a leaf from the porch before looking at her again. "Kevin has aplastic anemia. A bone marrow transplant is the only thing that can save him at this point, and I'm—"

"The donor." At least now things were beginning to make sense.

"The procedure's at 10:00 a.m. tomorrow at the university hospital's transplant center," he said. "I just wanted you to know."

She smiled around her own fear of sitting in a waiting room, counting down the minutes until she knew he was okay. "I'll be there."

He looked clearly surprised. "You don't have to do that, Erica."

"Do you want me there?"

"Yes, but I don't want you to suffer because of my own selfishness."

How could she possibly refuse? "There's nothing selfish about wanting some support. I'll have plenty of time to clear my schedule."

"As long as you're sure." He looked as if he wanted to say something more but only offered, "I'd better go. I have to be at the hospital early."

She wanted to hold him. She wanted to invite him in. She wanted more than he might be willing to give her. "I'll see you in the morning then."

When Erica turned to go inside, Kieran was right there at her back, his palm preventing her from opening the door. "I know I don't have the right to ask, but God, I want to stay with you tonight."

She slowly faced him, one important question weighing heavily on her mind. "Do you want a warm body, or do you want me?"

He tipped his forehead against hers. "It's not about sex, Erica. I need to be with you. I need you more than I've ever needed anyone. "

And that was all she needed to hear. Wordlessly, she clasped his hand and once in the house, tossed the gift on the sofa before leading him into the bedroom where she guided him to the bed. They stood face-to-face, neither moving for a time, until Erica took control by pulling his shirt over his head. The chemistry that had always existed between them took over, beginning with a harried dispersal of clothing and ending with them both naked and entwined across the bed. Kieran's touch was gentle, but his kiss was almost desperate. "I can't get close enough to you," he told her, though it wasn't long before they were as close as they could possibly be.

Their lovemaking was as passionate as before, as strong as Erica had ever known. And she was as lost in him as she'd been the first time. After their bodies calmed, Kieran rested his head on her breast, and she cradled it in her arms. When she felt the dampness against her skin, she knew that he'd finally given up the battle to be brave. Tears never came easy or often for a man like Kieran, and for that reason Erica cherished them all the more. Loved him all the more.

Then she did the one thing that he had done for her their first night together. She held him close, stroked his hair and whispered, "Everything's going to be okay."

* * *

Erica was anything but okay. With every step she took toward the hospital's entry, her breath came faster and harder. Her palms began to perspire, her head began to spin. But she had to keep moving despite her anxiety. She was already late. Maybe even too late to see Kieran before they took him away for the procedure. Before she had a chance to tell him she loved him, something she should have done before he'd left at dawn. She refused to think about that now, or invite anything negative into her world.

Immediately outside the sliding-glass doors, Erica paused long enough to give herself a good pep talk, to establish some sort of calm before she faced Kieran's family. This wasn't the same hospital where Stormy had undergone her numerous surgeries. This wasn't the same emergency room where Jeff had died. This was a totally different situation, a totally different patient. But it was still a hospital.

Somehow she managed to make it to the second floor without hyperventilating in the elevator, and she was able to find the sign pointing to surgery without needing assistance. She also managed a pleasant look when Mallory approached her. "Erica, I'm so glad you're here. I tried to call you, but I didn't have your phone number."

A surge of panic threatened to strip Erica of any composure. "What's wrong?"

Mallory hooked her arm through Erica's and began guiding her toward the waiting area. "Nothing's wrong. They took Kieran in early because the case before his cancelled. He's already been in the O.R. for almost an hour."

Leave it to Kieran to somehow save her from the excruciating waiting game, although Erica recognized he'd had nothing to do with it. When they reached the bank of chairs housing the majority of the O'Brien clan, Kieran's mother caught sight of Erica and rushed over. "I'm so glad you've joined us, dear. I know how important it is to Kieran that you've come."

Erica hugged Lucy, all the while thinking how nice it was to find someone who hit her eye level. "I'm sorry I'm late. I would have been here sooner but I was stuck in the middle of the Interstate because of a fender bender. I can't believe I didn't get to see him before he went in."

Lucy patted her cheek. "You can see him when he's ready for visitors."

"And it looks like that could be now." Mallory nodded to Erica's right where Devin O'Brien emerged from a lengthy corridor. The group gathered round, anxiously awaiting news, but no one was more anxious than Erica.

"He's in recovery now," Devin said. "Everything went fine. He's just waking up, and he's going to have a sore a—"

"Don't say it, young man," Lucy admonished.

"A sore butt," Devin said, looking suitably scolded. "He also had a slight drop in his blood pressure during the procedure, so they'll keep him in recovery for a while longer to make sure he's stable."

Erica's own pressure most likely bottomed out over the news and when Lucy said, "Oh, heavens," Devin held up a hand to silence her. "He's okay, Mom. He was never in any real danger."

Erica questioned whether the fates were testing her, cruelly standing by to see if she might buckle under the pressure. Thing was, she'd passed the test. She hadn't panicked, hadn't jumped to unnecessary conclusions. Hadn't rushed out the door in search of air. Her only concern was seeing Kieran.

But after Devin said, "Two family members at a time can go in now," Erica thought she'd been ruled out, until he added, "And he wants to see Erica first."

She looked around to find everyone grinning at her. "But I'm not family."

Lucy patted her cheek. "As far as we're concerned, you are. Now go tell our boy we'll see him soon."

Without further argument, Erica followed Devin through the double doors indicating the recovery unit, this time excitement dogging her steps. Outside the cubicle, he told her, "He's still out of it, so don't be surprised if he talks out of his head."

Erica didn't care what he said, or if he said anything at all. She only wanted to make certain he was okay. "I'll just stay a few minutes so everyone else can have their turn."

Devin presented the patent O'Brien smile. "Take your time. You're the one he wants to see."

Erica brushed past the plaid curtain and took her place beside the narrow bed. Kieran's eyes were closed against the overhead light, his lips slightly parted and his jaw surrounded by the usual dark shading. Even in the ridiculous cap covering his hair, he still looked beautiful.

When she took his hand, his lids drifted open and he smiled. "You're here."

"Yes, I'm here. How do you feel?"

"Like my head's not attached to my body."

"Nice shower cap," she said. "Mind if I take a picture with my camera phone?"

"Hell, no."

When he tried to sit up, Erica nudged him back down. "Don't move, Kieran. You might hurt something."

He grimaced and gritted his teeth. "I feel like someone used my kidneys as a punching bag."

She brushed her knuckles over his rough cheek. "When you get out of this place, I'll rub it and make it better."

He curled his hand around her neck and reeled her close. "Feel free to climb in bed with me and get my mind off my pain."

"If I do that, I'm liable to get tossed out and we'll both have sore backsides. Will a little kiss do?"

"Oh, yeah." For a man under the influence of anesthesia, he didn't miss a beat with that kiss, and it was anything but little. In fact, it went a bit beyond the point of respectability for a hospital setting, the only reason Erica ended the kiss first.

"You're well on your way to recovery, Kieran O'Brien."

"And I love you, Erica Stevens."

Erica swallowed hard around the shock. "You're drunk."

"I'm serious."

If his expression was any indication, he was. "I love you, too," she said. "Although you probably won't remember any of this in an hour." Yet she would never forget it. She also hoped he said it again when he was completely coherent.

He ran his fingertip along her jaw, his eyes looking heavy. "Since I'm wearing a butt-exposing gown and a shower cap, I'm not going to propose to you right now. But one of these days…"

After Kieran's eyes closed again, Erica kissed his cheek. She had no idea if he would recall what he'd said or if it was only the drugs doing the talking. But maybe one of these days…

Epilogue

Erica loved summer days best, and this particular Saturday morning in early June was picture-perfect. She waited at the Porsche for Kieran and Stormy to finish gathering softball equipment from the dugout, thrilled with the progress her daughter had made as a relief pitcher for the softball team. An exceptional athlete, the coach had told Erica at the last practice. Jeff would be so proud of her, Erica thought as she watched Kieran and Stormy work their way through the remaining family members and fans. The memories of her former husband came less frequently now, but always fondly. She would forever reserve a special place in her heart for Jeff. She would always be grateful to him for giving her a precious child. In many ways, she would always love him.

But she also loved another man who'd been an important part of her life for the past seven months. And Kieran loved her, too, something he told her often while completely coherent. He hadn't spoken of proposing since that day in the hospital, but as far as Erica was concerned, that was okay. Whatever happened, happened. Right now she looked forward to spending the weekend in Galveston, as they had most every weekend since May.

With her baseball cap turned backward and her face dotted with dirt, Stormy rushed over like a tempest, doing her name justice. "Did you see me strike out that girl, Mom?"

"Yes, sweetie, I did. Your and Mallory's hard work has really paid off."

Kieran walked up to the pair and laid a palm on Stormy's head. "Did you ask your mom yet?"

Erica frowned. "Ask me what?"

Stormy exchanged a look with Kieran before she turned her attention back to Erica. "Grandma Lucy wants me to help her babysit the twins this weekend instead of going to the beach house. Can I?"

Stormy loved the beach, but she also loved the O'Brien babies. And that baby love would allow Erica some rare alone time with Kieran. "Sounds fine to me, if you're sure it's okay with Lucy to have you two whole days."

"It's okay," Kieran said. "Mallory's still here, talking to Stormy's coach. She's offered to drop her off before she heads out of town with Whit for the weekend."

Stormy gave Erica a brief hug. "See you Monday, Mom," she said before she sprinted off toward Mallory.

Kieran winked at her. "Guess it's you and me and the beach all weekend, all alone. No more sneaking around to make out."

Erica got a case of the chills just thinking about it. "What are we waiting for?"

"Not a damn thing."

Kieran drove out of the parking lot slowly but hit the accelerator the minute he'd cleared all the other cars and kids. Erica was still getting used to his occasional need for speed, although he had learned to show much more restraint, at least when it came to his driving. When it came to lovemaking, well…

After they were on their way out of Houston, Erica shifted in her seat as far as the belt would allow. "Did you hear the news? Stormy tells me Candice has a new boyfriend. A very rich new boyfriend, according to Lisa."

"A merger made in heaven," Kieran muttered. "How's Lisa taking it?"

"Stormy claims she's okay. The man bought Lisa some kind of show pony and that seems to have made her happy. I sometimes worry about her influence on Stormy, though. But I guess I can't choose her friends."

Kieran reached over the console and laid a hand on her thigh. "Look at it this way. Stormy's probably a better influence on Lisa."

"That's what I'm hoping."

He took his eyes from the road and gave her a long once-over. "Did I tell you how great you look today?"

"Did I tell you you're about to miss the exit?"

He crossed two lanes of traffic and turned off in the nick of time. "That top you're wearing is distracting me."

"It's tasteful and covers enough." And it showed her arms, something she'd only recently been brave enough to do in public. But with all the strength training, she'd gained some mighty fine definition. And she hadn't gained a pound since she'd dropped twenty-five, a number Kieran had convinced her she should be happy with. She was happy. Ecstatic even. Besides, he remained rather fond of her butt, a good thing since it obviously wasn't going to magically shrink.

"You made quite an impact today on the men in the stands," Kieran continued. "When you stood up to go get the popcorn, even Logan commented on how good you look, right before Jenna punched him in the ribs. After that, Logan said pregnancy has made Jenna moody, and horny. She punched him again. It was great."

Erica laughed. "Your brothers spend more time in hot water with their wives than out of it." She considered one particular O'Brien brother that wasn't far from any of their thoughts these days. "How was Kevin when you saw him yesterday?"

"He's better, at least physically. He's getting ready to move into the house Whit designed. I never thought I'd see Kev living in a house in the burbs."

"I guess he's decided to settle down."

"By himself, maybe. He only leaves the house to have lunch with us on Sunday. He hasn't mentioned a woman, and that's not the norm at all. As bad as he was before, sometimes I'd like to see a glimpse of the old Kevin." He smiled, a sad one. "Never thought I'd say that, either."

Erica reached over and patted Kieran's arm. "Give him time. Facing death changes a person. Someone will come along and give him his life back."

Kieran took her hand and brought it to his lips for a kiss. "If he's as lucky as me, that's a possibility."

At times like these, Erica counted her own blessings. Kieran had become much more open in recent months, and although he would never be the kind of man who spouted poetry on a whim, he did have his moments, and this was one of them.

As soon as they crossed the causeway into Galveston, Kieran turned on his blinker to exit. "I want to show you the progress they've made on the new club before we head to the beach. Looks like it might be ready for a July grand opening."

The last time Erica had seen the building, it had been a maze of massive, unfinished caverns covered in sheetrock.

"I'm looking forward to it, as long as we don't stay too long. I'm ready to relax on the beach."

He sent her that look, the one that said he had some innovative ideas on his mind. "The sandy one or the one in the bedroom?"

"Both. We could take advantage of that dune behind the house."

"This will take ten minutes, tops. Five if we hurry."

Kieran whipped into the parking lot, shut off the engine and practically pulled Erica out of the car before she could draw a breath. Once inside, he took her by the hand and bypassed the elaborate lobby before pushing through a pair of heavy wood grain double doors. Erica expected to see a room full of state-of-the-art exercise equipment. But never in a zillion years did she predict she'd be looking at balance beams and parallel bars. She could only stand there like a sculpture, speechless, until Kieran asked, "What do you think?"

"This is incredible." She tore her gaze away to look at the man responsible for the surprise. "But what on earth made you decide to add a gymnastics studio?"

He slid his arms around her. "I thought it would be a good business venture. The parents can work out while the kids take lessons. And since I happen to know a former gymnast who's always wanted to teach…"

Erica backed out of his arms and held up her hands, as if to fend him off. "Wait a minute. I haven't done anything remotely resembling gymnastics for over ten years. I'm not qualified to teach."

"You can do anything you set your mind to, Erica. You've proved that to me over and over again."

Erica surveyed the room and remembered how much satisfaction she'd experienced when she'd had a particularly good practice. How much fun she'd had during her gymnastics days. Kieran was offering her the answer to an unrealized dream, and all she had to do was accept the gift with grace. She strolled around for a few moments, trying to picture herself guiding students to their full potential, as she had been guided once upon a long time ago. But when she spotted the rings suspended from the ceiling, she said, "If I agree to do this, you're going to have to hire someone to train the boys. I don't do the rings."

"I've already taken care of that. The question is, will you do this ring?"

Erica turned to find Kieran holding up an emerald cut diamond solitaire flashing bright beneath the overhead lights. To counteract the sudden threat of tears, she said, "If you intend to hang it from the ceiling, it's not quite big enough to hold me up."

He cracked a crooked grin. "I intend to put it on your hand, but only if you'll marry me."

She crossed the room and practically hurled herself into his arms, shouting, "Yes!" She didn't care that she started sobbing like a baby when Kieran slipped the ring on her finger. She didn't care about anything when he followed the promise with the sweetest of kisses. She only cared that "one of these days" had finally arrived.

He pulled back and thumbed away a tear. "Are you going to be okay?"

More okay than she'd been in quite some time. "Sure. I'm just prone to fits of emotion when I'm happy. You should see me when I'm pregnant."

"I plan on seeing you that way at least three times."

Three? Lord, she couldn't begin to imagine that. "One more."

"Two."

"Deal." She was so certain that they were doing the right thing, but she wanted Kieran to be sure, too. "You realize we're not always going to get along this well."

"I know. You're going to get angry with me when I shut down."

"And you're going to get frustrated when I won't shut up."

"I love you, Erica. Even your faults. Especially your faults."

The honesty in his eyes told her he spoke from the heart. "We'll both do well to remember marriage is always a work in progress, even when it's not perfect. And heaven knows I'm anything but perfect."

Kieran kissed her again, softly, sincerely, sealing the deal. "As far as I'm concerned, Erica Stevens, you're as close to perfect as it gets."

CELEBRATE
60 YEARS
OF PURE READING PLEASURE
WITH **HARLEQUIN**®!

We'll be spotlighting a different series
every month throughout 2009
to celebrate our 60th anniversary.

Look for Harlequin® Blaze™ in March!

0-60

After all, a lot can happen in 60 years,
or 60 minutes...or 60 seconds!

Find out what's going down in Blaze's
heart-stopping new miniseries *0-60!*
Getting from "Hello" to "How was it?"
can happen fast....

Look for the brand-new 0-60 miniseries in March 2009!

HARLEQUIN® *Romance*®

This February the Harlequin® Romance series
will feature six Diamond Brides stories featuring
diamond proposals and gorgeous grooms.

Share your dream wedding proposal and you could WIN!

The most romantic entry will win a diamond
necklace and will inspire a proposal in one of
our upcoming Diamond Grooms books in 2010.

In 100 words or less, tell us the most romantic
way that you dream of being proposed to.

For more information, and to enter
the Diamond Brides Proposal contest, please visit
www.DiamondBridesProposal.com

Or mail your entry to us at:

IN THE U.S.: 3010 Walden Ave., P.O. Box 9069, Buffalo, NY 14269-9069
IN CANADA: 225 Duncan Mill Road, Don Mills, ON M3B 3K9

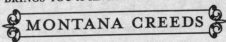

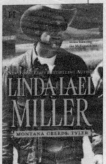

REQUEST YOUR FREE BOOKS!

2 FREE NOVELS PLUS 2 FREE GIFTS!

SPECIAL EDITION®

Life, Love and Family!

YES! Please send me 2 FREE Silhouette Special Edition® novels and my 2 FREE gifts (gifts are worth about $10). After receiving them, if I don't wish to receive any more books, I can return the shipping statement marked "cancel." If I don't cancel, I will receive 6 brand-new novels every month and be billed just $4.24 per book in the U.S. or $4.99 per book in Canada, plus 25¢ shipping and handling per book and applicable taxes, if any*. That's a savings of at least 15% off the cover price! I understand that accepting the 2 free books and gifts places me under no obligation to buy anything. I can always return a shipment and cancel at any time. Even if I never buy another book from Silhouette, the two free books and gifts are mine to keep forever.

235 SDN EEYU 335 SDN EEY6

Name	(PLEASE PRINT)	
Address		Apt. #
City	State/Prov.	Zip/Postal Code

Signature (if under 18, a parent or guardian must sign)

Mail to the Silhouette Reader Service:
IN U.S.A.: P.O. Box 1867, Buffalo, NY 14240-1867
IN CANADA: P.O. Box 609, Fort Erie, Ontario L2A 5X3

Not valid to current subscribers of Silhouette Special Edition books.

Want to try two free books from another line?
Call 1-800-873-8635 or visit www.morefreebooks.com.

* Terms and prices subject to change without notice. N.Y. residents add applicable sales tax. Canadian residents will be charged applicable provincial taxes and GST. Offer not valid in Quebec. This offer is limited to one order per household. All orders subject to approval. Credit or debit balances in a customer's account(s) may be offset by any other outstanding balance owed by or to the customer. Please allow 4 to 6 weeks for delivery. Offer available while quantities last.

Your Privacy: Silhouette is committed to protecting your privacy. Our Privacy Policy is available online at www.eHarlequin.com or upon request from the Reader Service. From time to time we make our lists of customers available to reputable third parties who may have a product or service of interest to you. If you would prefer we not share your name and address, please check here. ☐

SSE08R

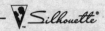

SPECIAL EDITION

TRAVIS'S APPEAL

by *USA TODAY* bestselling author
MARIE FERRARELLA

Shana O'Reilly couldn't deny it—family lawyer
Travis Marlowe had some kind of appeal. But
as Travis handled her father's tricky estate
planning, he discovered things weren't what
they seemed in the O'Reilly clan. Would
an explosive secret leave Travis and Shana's
budding relationship in tatters?

*Available March 2009
wherever books are sold.*

The Inside Romance newsletter has a NEW look for the new year!

Same great content, brand-new look!

The Inside Romance newsletter is a FREE quarterly newsletter highlighting our upcoming series releases and promotions!

Click on the Inside Romance link on the front page of
www.eHarlequin.com or e-mail us at
insideromance@harlequin.ca to sign up
to receive your FREE newsletter today!

You can also subscribe by writing to us at: HARLEQUIN BOOKS
Attention: Customer Service Department
P.O. Box 9057, Buffalo, NY 14269-9057

Please allow 4-6 weeks for delivery of the first issue by mail.

IRNNEW09

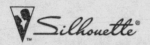

COMING NEXT MONTH

Available February 24, 2009

#1957 TRIPLE TROUBLE—Lois Faye Dyer
Fortunes of Texas: Return to Red Rock
Financial analyst Nick Fortune was a whiz at numbers, not diapers.
So after tragedy forced him to assume guardianship of triplets, he
was clueless—until confident Charlene London became their nanny.
That's when Nick fell for Charlene, and the trouble really began!

#1958 TRAVIS'S APPEAL—Marie Ferrarella
Kate's Boys
Shana O'Reilly couldn't deny it—family lawyer Travis Marlowe
had some kind of appeal. But as Travis handled her father's tricky
estate planning, he discovered things weren't what they seemed in the
O'Reilly clan. Would an explosive secret leave Travis and Shana's
budding relationship in tatters?

#1959 A TEXAN ON HER DOORSTEP—Stella Bagwell
Famous Families
More Famous Families from Special Edition! Abandoned by his
mother, shafted by his party-girl ex-wife, cynical Texas lawman
Mac McCleod was over love. Until a chance reunion with his mother
in a hospital, and a choice introduction to her intriguing doctor,
Ileana Murdock, changed everything....

#1960 MARRYING THE VIRGIN NANNY—Teresa Southwick
The Nanny Network
Billionaire Jason Garrett would pay a premium to the Nanny Network
for a caregiver for his infant son, Brady. And luckily, sweet, innocent
nanny Maggie Shepherd instantly bonded with father and son, giving
Jason a priceless new lease on love.

#1961 LULLABY FOR TWO—Karen Rose Smith
The Baby Experts
When Vince Rossi assumed custody of his friend's baby son after an
accident, the little boy was hurt, and if it weren't for Dr. Tessa McGuire,
Vince wouldn't know which end was up. Sure, Tessa was Vince's
ex-wife and they had a rocky history, but as they bonded over the boy,
could it be they had a future—together—too?

#1962 CLAIMING THE RANCHER'S HEART—Cindy Kirk
Footloose Stacie Collins had a knack for matchmaking. After inheriting
her grandma's home in Montana, she and two gal pals decided to
head for the hills and test their theories of love on the locals. When
their "scientific" survey yielded Josh Collins as Stacie's ideal beau, it
must have been a computer error—or was this rugged rancher really a
perfect match?

SSECNMBPA0209